Praise for Jos

"Taut and emotionally wrenching … I couldn't put [*Albatross*] down. Josie Bloss is an author to watch."
—Meg Cabot, author of *The Princess Diaries* and the Airhead series

"[*Albatross* is] a startlingly realistic portrayal of emotionally abusive relationships." —*School Library Journal*

"Bloss's descriptions of lust and envy are honest and captivating." —*Publishers Weekly*

"Tess's story will wrench hearts." —*Kirkus Reviews*

"Refreshingly real and honest." —*KLIATT*

"[*Band Geek Love*] features a memorable cast of characters that jump off the page." —*SLJTeen*

"Hits all of the right notes … Josie Bloss's [*Band Geek Love*] will be music to your ears."
—Slayground.livejournal.com

"I immediately loved [*Band Geek Love*] … it's so much fun." —TeensReadToo.com

"[*Band Geek Love*] is a realistic, intriguing story."
—BloodyYank.blogspot.com

FAKING FAITH

Also by Josie Bloss
Band Geek Love
Band Geeked Out
Albatross

FAKING FAITH

JOSIE BLOSS

Woodbury, Minnesota

First Edition
Second Printing, 2011

Book Design by Bob Gaul
Cover design by Ellen Lawson
Cover image © iStockphoto.com/Famke Backx
 Back cover image © Photo Disc

Flux, an imprint of Llewellyn Worldwide Ltd.

Library of Congress Cataloging-in-Publication Data
Bloss, Josie, 1981–
 Faking Faith / Josie Bloss.—1st ed.
  p. cm.
 Summary: After a humiliating incident involving some bad decisions on her part, seventeen-year-old Dylan discovers the blogs of fundamentalist Christian girls and starts passing herself off as one of them in her own blog, leading her to some unexpected insights about herself and her values.
 ISBN 978-0-7387-2757-8
[1. Fundamentalism—Fiction. 2. Christian life—Fiction. 3. Impostors and imposture—Fiction. 4. Conduct of life—Fiction.] I. Title.
 PZ7.B6238Fak 2012
 [Fic]—dc23

                                            2011022348

Flux
Llewellyn Worldwide Ltd.
2143 Wooddale Drive
Woodbury, MN 55125-2989
www.fluxnow.com

Acknowledgments

Gratitude and appreciation for my wonderful agent, Kate Schafer Testerman, and to everyone at Flux who helped *Faking Faith* become a reality. It's been a pleasure and a privilege to work with all of you.

Special thanks go to the kind people who read early drafts of my weird Internet-obsession book, including Kelly Johnson, Emily Goodson, Kathleen Walker, Gayle Gingrich, and Mark Kaley.

And I give endless thanks, as always, to my amazing extended family. Your encouragement and support has meant so much.

For Alyssa and Emily, the best stepsisters

ONE

School was the same sort of hell every day.

I went to homeroom and everyone ignored me. I went through my morning classes, everyone ignored me. I ate my lunch alone in a library study carrel (secretly, so the librarian wouldn't yell at me about getting crumbs in the keyboard), and tried to do homework. Afternoon classes, more of the same. Ignored.

And then home. Where I was also mostly ignored. In some grim way, I sort of appreciated the consistency.

People still hissed "psycho slut" or "crazy bitch" at me in the hallways, of course. It happened less often as the months wore on, but still enough to make me feel a little insane and perpetually paranoid as I walked past groups of people on my solitary way to class. But really, most of my day was ghostly and quiet.

It used to be different. I used to be busy—with dance

classes and piano lessons and other activities typical of an over-scheduled, high-achieving suburban Chicago high school student.

And I used to have a couple of kickass best friends— Kelsey and Amanda. The kind of friends who would stay on the phone with me until midnight, endlessly analyzing the nuances of a conversation with some crush. Who would lend me shirts and borrow my shoes and offer blunt opinions on my hair. Who had known all my secrets since fourth grade. Who would walk with me, arms linked, through the school halls between classes.

Kelsey and Amanda and I had been a solid mass, an indivisible force to be reckoned with. Even if we weren't part of the most popular crowd, we could hold our own in the high school hierarchy. If you messed with one of us, you messed with all of us. I didn't even know how great I had it.

Because now I was alone at the bottom, and my old friends ignored me like everyone else. Except for when I was being taunted, I might as well not have existed. For anyone, anywhere.

The thing is, I deserved it. Even though I still couldn't admit it out loud, I knew for certain that I deserved everything that came to me. I had been so stupid.

. . .

Blake Compton hit on me at a party last September.

At first, I'd been sure it was a joke.

Blake was one of those unattainable hot guys who seem

to glide through the world like they run the place, oozing privilege and self-satisfaction out of every pore. He was the guy who nearly every girl lusted after, even the girls who rolled their eyes and claimed his player reputation made him ugly. He knew just how to work his charm and make anyone crumble to his will with one raised dark eyebrow or half a lazy smile. Blake could make people powerless.

As a girl with a serious appreciation for the male form, I'd adored Blake Compton from afar since freshman year. I'd typed a series of humiliating entries in my journal about the exact glossy brown shade of his perfectly messy hair and the precise gold of his perpetually tanned skin. I'd even written a terrible poem about the shape of his lips and that little quirk in the corner of his mouth that made me feel shivery in the knees whenever I caught sight of him in the hallways.

But I didn't have any illusions that I'd ever have a chance with him or anything.

I thought I was probably everyday-pretty and smart enough to get by okay in the world, but boys like Blake are attracted to the sparkliest girls. The gorgeous girls who also glide through the world like they own the place. And I was wholly resigned to the fact that I'd always be admiring the Blake Comptons of the universe from across the room where I belonged.

It was just the order of things.

But then suddenly there he was, in the flesh, standing right next to me at Caitlin Merriweather's back-to-school party. Quirking his mouth. At me. And everything changed.

"Dylan, right?" he said.

I nodded dumbly, resisting the urge to glance around to see if this was a prank. Blake Compton knew who I was?

"Hey, you know, I always thought that was a cool name. Can I get you another drink or three?" was all he had to say, with that lazy, heart-stopping smile.

By the end of the night I was drunker than I'd ever been in my life, and had been easily persuaded to accompany Blake to one of the bedrooms upstairs to "spend some time alone." Kelsey and Amanda texted me a half million times from downstairs, but I ignored my vibrating phone. This was bliss, heaven. A cute boy, *the* cute boy, with his tongue in my ear.

Okay, so he really wasn't the best kisser in the whole world, and he was a lot more handsy than I was totally comfortable with, but he was *Blake Compton*. He smelled like expensive spicy cologne and confidence.

As he kissed me, I felt like I drifted out of my body and hovered somewhere up near the ceiling, watching the two of us on the bed below. I couldn't believe it was happening to me.

Guys in general had always made me kind of nervous and marble-mouthed, and I felt like a jackass every time I tried to flirt. At that point, I'd only kissed two boys at parties, mostly just to get the experience out of the way. Meanwhile, Amanda and Kelsey, who seemed to have some secret knowledge that I'd missed out on, had already racked up five boyfriends between them. They were just barely virgins anymore, and both knew far more then I did about the male species.

So I guess I expected them to be happy for me as we started to hike the mile back to my house for the planned post-party sleepover. Or at least good-naturedly teasing about Blake choosing me out of the masses.

"He said that we should hang out," I said, still tipsy on my heels and giddy with my good luck. "Like a date...a real date! I mean, I know he has a reputation for being a player, but he said he really likes me and he sounded so...*real*."

Some small part of me realized I was being an idiot. My friends obviously felt this too, and they both gave me dubious looks that I chose to ignore.

I continued babbling. "And you guys were totally right about this shirt! He said I looked really hot in it."

I glanced down to admire the gauzy piece of form-fitting fabric that Amanda had lent to me earlier in the night. It was the first time in my life I'd ever felt cuter than my friends, who I'd always secretly thought were much more stylish and magazine-pretty than me.

Not that they made me feel that way on purpose. It was just the way things were.

"Dude, Dylan," said Kelsey, who was short, feisty, and prided herself on never sugarcoating a damn thing. "Everyone knows Blake's an ass. He goes through girls like toilet paper. He's just going to use you."

"What?" I said. "You're crazy."

"No, for serious, we're not just saying that," said

Amanda, in a surprisingly firm tone considering she was one of those sweet-voiced girls who seems to talk solely in question marks. She was compulsively wrapping her long brown hair around her index finger like she always did when she was upset. "Blake is totally bad news. You know that, right?"

I stopped walking and blinked at them in disbelief.

"What, you don't think someone like him would want to be with me?" I said, my hands on my hips. "I'm not good enough or something? Is that it? Jealous much?"

In hindsight, I'd come to realize this was not my best moment. In fact, it was possibly the dictionary definition of my worst moment ever. The moment I'd later turn over and over in my mind while cringing and wishing like hell for a time machine so I could go back and slap myself.

Kelsey and Amanda gaped at me, and then Kelsey stormed back toward the party with a muttered "*dumbass*."

"No one said that you weren't good enough! Look, Dylan, we just want you to be careful because we love you," Amanda said, glancing after Kelsey with a frown. "I mean, you've never hooked up with a guy like him before, and—"

"And what?" I spat back. "You think I don't know what I'm doing?"

Amanda looked down at the ground and shrugged. It was plain unavoidable fact that I was the least experienced of the three of us, which was something that I'd readily admit to on a normal day.

But on that night, I was drunk and defensive and

didn't see why anyone had to throw my innocence in my face. Just because the hottest guy in the school happened to decide that he liked me instead of one of them? Just because neither of them were currently hooking up with anyone? Just because I was the one getting some attention, like that was the craziest thing that could ever happen?

"When I need your advice, I'll ask for it!" I said, crossing my arms tightly over my chest, irrational anger building in my throat at the sight of Amanda's stricken face.

"Dylan—"

"I'm sick of being your tag-along ugly friend! You just keep me around to feel better about yourselves," I burst out, then turned my back on Amanda's shocked expression. "Just go. Go back to the party and leave me alone. You guys suck."

Even as I said it, I knew I was wrong. And I hated myself.

"But Dylan…" I heard Amanda say tearfully as I stalked away toward my house.

"Just let her go," snapped Kelsey from down the street, where she'd been watching us. "She's out of her mind."

And that was the last time I talked to either of them. I was That Girl who let a stupid guy get between her and her best friends.

T W O

Blake and I lasted for two months.

At the beginning, it was awesome. For the first time in my life, I was a tangential member of the truly popular crowd. I wasn't actual friends with anyone else in that circle, but as Blake's girlfriend I got to sit at the big kids' table and was invited to the smaller and more exclusive drunken gatherings. Even though the girls in the group barely tolerated my sudden presence and sometimes said catty things right to my face, at least I wasn't outright ignored.

And then Blake would twine his arm around my waist and put his face in my hair as we walked through the crowded halls, and it was perfection. I felt desired and whole by his side, like I had found my one true place in the world and that was all that mattered.

Everything else in my life swiftly fell away. I quit my dance classes, which I had been taking since I was five.

I stopped showing up to piano lessons. National Honor Society meetings and volunteering seemed like a waste of time now that I had a boyfriend to make out with after school. My grades slowly started sinking. I got my first-ever C on an English essay.

"Nerd," Blake said when I told him.

My parents fought me for a while, harping on discipline and my future and college applications in that clueless, tone-deaf way old people have. But they were both partners at a big law firm in the city and it's not like they had time to monitor exactly what I was doing every minute of the day. Eventually, with huge sighs of deep disappointment, they stopped bringing it up. I was happily lost in Blake.

Whenever I saw Kelsey or Amanda in the hall, I looked pointedly away and pretended like they didn't exist.

Of course, they didn't try to talk to me either. I sometimes caught Amanda giving me one of her wide-eyed, wounded-animal looks, but she never actually tried to talk to me. And I got the distinct impression that Kelsey wouldn't even stop to spit on me if I were on fire.

Sometimes I wished we could all just get over it and be friends again, because deep down, below my pride and hurt feelings and Blake bliss, I really missed them. And I had questions. I didn't realize relationships could move as fast as mine and Blake's seemed to be moving. But every time I thought seriously about trying to make up with them and admit I'd been irrational, I got pissed off at what they'd said the night of the party. At how unsupportive and doubtful and dismissive they'd been.

And shouldn't my awesomely hot and devoted boyfriend be enough for me? Hadn't he proven that he wasn't just using me, that this was something good and real?

My friends had been wrong, and they were still refusing to admit to it.

"You don't need those jealous bitches," Blake said after I told him the story, wrapping my ponytail around his wrist and pulling gently. "You're better off without them anyway."

And I'd agreed.

Blake was my first everything.

After we had been dating for only two weeks, he yanked me close and told me he couldn't stand it anymore, that it was cruel and unusual punishment to make him wait. He wanted to make love to me so bad it physically hurt. That's exactly what he said—"make love." It sounded lovely and romantic to me. Just like what a first time should be.

And I was flattered and thrilled, and tried to pretend I wasn't freaked out by the fact that it had only been a few weeks since he'd first talked to me. I decided that I *must* love him, because I wanted him too. It had to be love, right? This whirlwind feeling of wanting to be as close to him as possible? Wanting to make him happy in any way that I could?

So he snuck into my room—well, technically, he just walked into it on a night when both my parents were working late—with a bottle of vodka and a condom from his wallet.

It was awkward and kind of painful and much

quicker than I thought it would be. It didn't feel particularly like love. More like something perfunctory and unexciting and biological.

Though he seemed to enjoy it enough.

After Blake kissed my cheek and left, I curled up in my bed and stared at my phone, which was sitting on the pillow next to me. I wished more than anything I could talk to someone about what had happened and get some perspective on my experience. But there wasn't one person in the whole world I felt like I could call.

One weekend when Blake was in Colorado skiing with his brother, he drunk-dialed me. He was flirting hard and things got a little heated up. Eventually he started trying to talk me into taking a couple of topless pictures of myself with my webcam and emailing them to his phone. And I wanted him to love me so much that I did it, even though I felt ridiculous and kind of gross.

It took me fifteen attempts to get the angle right.

"You'd never share these with anyone, right?" I said, hesitating for a moment before I hit send. "I mean, this is just between us?"

"'Course! Who do you think I am?" he said, a smile in his slurred voice. "Now I'll never be away from you, baby. You're so good to me."

Obviously, I should have known.

. . .

My relationship with Blake ended horrifically, of course, as anyone other than me could have predicted.

In November, Blake started acting chilly and distant. He wouldn't return my texts for hours and mostly ignored me at lunch, angling away at the cafeteria table so I'd have to make conversation with the girls who didn't like me. He'd give me improbable excuses about why he couldn't come over to my house, even on the opportune nights when both my parents were gone. He stopped walking with me through the halls.

I ignored the ache in my stomach and excused Blake's behavior away for as long as possible. It was just a weird boy phase, I rationalized, trying not to give in to the panic. He'd get over whatever his problem was and things would go back to how they were before. We'd date until we graduated, and then go to the same college and get married when we were twenty-four before he started business school, and live happily ever after.

And then one day after school, I caught Blake making out with Caitlin Merriweather up against his Range Rover.

He always gave me a ride home, so clearly he'd meant for me to find them together. He just didn't care anymore.

I stopped for a moment, watching how his hand moved up her arm to cup her shoulder. Observing, in a distant and almost academic sort of way, how his mouth moved over her lips in a gross swallowing motion that reminded me of a snake devouring its prey. I idly wondered if it looked ugly like that when we kissed.

When we used to kiss…when I used to have a boy-friend…

Then my vision started throbbing red, like every cell in my body was about to explode. I completely lost my sanity right on the spot.

"You cheating asshole!" I'd screamed, and they stopped kissing and looked at me. I threw my messenger bag at his head, and Caitlin shrieked like a little girl. Blake blocked my bag with his forearm and broke away from her.

"Damn, Dylan, chill out," Blake started to say, rolling his eyes, his palms up as if I were a diseased wild animal. People in the parking lot were beginning to stop and watch the drama, their mouths hanging open.

"Excuse me? I will definitely *not* chill out! How could you do this to me?"

"Dylan…come on, be reasonable. We had a good run, right? It was never going to last, you knew that."

In response, I went around to open the back of Blake's Range Rover, where I knew he kept his golf clubs, and yanked out his nine iron. I gripped it firmly and turned to face him. The crowd gasped appreciatively. I dimly registered that a kid from my physics class was holding up his phone, recording the whole thing.

"Hey…uh, hey, what the hell are you doing?" Blake was actually smiling, like he thought it was a big joke. No girl had ever dared touch his sacred golf clubs in anger.

I looked him in his beautiful eyes, rage filling me to the brim. My friends had been right. I was an idiot. Of course he'd betray me like this after everything I'd so easily given to him. My time, my life, my *body*.

My hands quivered around the golf club, and for a moment, I felt powerful.

"I'm doing this, you asshole!"

Without another thought, I bashed off his side-view mirror. Then I started smashing away at the windshield with every ounce of strength, watching the glass spiderweb, until Blake ripped the club out of my hands and shoved me away. As I stood there gasping for breath, already starting to regret what I'd just done, Blake slowly walked up to me. He put his face so close to mine, it almost seemed like he was going to kiss me on the mouth.

"I only hung around with you because I knew you'd put out, you dumb little insecure bitch," he told me in a low voice, somehow both amused and furious. "You're pathetic. I'll end you."

Then he turned, put his arm around Caitlin, and walked away.

The next day, everyone who mattered at school had the topless webcam pictures of me in their inboxes from an anonymous email address. The email also contained a link to a YouTube video of me swinging at the car with the golf club. *Dylan Mahoney = CRAAAZY SLUT* was in the subject line.

I knew all that because it was forwarded on to me by several thoughtful acquaintances from Blake's lunch table.

At which point I fetal-positioned up in bed and prayed not to wake up.

I wasn't there to witness much of the immediate after-math because I got an immediate five-day suspension for the busted car—a punishment I'd expected. My parents, who both managed to take the morning off work to come deal with my screw-up, were able to convince Blake's screaming, red-faced father not to press charges.

But what really burned was getting called back into school two days later to get an additional suspension for the pictures.

My parents took another morning off and argued the sentence, but the administration at my school wanted to make an example of someone. "Sexting," as all the cable news shows breathlessly called it, was a trend the school district wanted to make a show of punishing, whatever the context. However unfair.

"But I only sent them to one person," I said to the vice principal, beyond tears in my humiliation. "I didn't *mean* for anyone else to see them. They were private pictures for my boyfriend!"

I looked desperately around the room for support, but my parents wouldn't even meet my glance. Dad sat with his hand covering his eyes, like he was denying what was happening right in front of him.

"Blake Compton says he lost his phone a few weeks ago and doesn't know anything about the pictures being disseminated. And unfortunately, there's no way to prove he had anything to do with it," the vice principal said, shaking his head. "Look, Dylan, you should just hope you don't get charged with distribution of child pornography, like some counties are doing. It doesn't matter what your intent was. You created and sent pictures of an underage girl. That's a felony."

I huddled back in my chair, wrapped my arms around myself, and shuddered. "But *I'm* the underage girl."

"It doesn't matter."

All anyone could do was shrug and frown at me like I was a lost cause.

My parents took me home, yelled at me for likely ruining my chances at a good college, and grounded me for the rest of the school year. Mom was particularly livid, like I had done this just to embarrass her personally.

"I can't believe you were so stupid!" she said, pacing the living room floor, almost in tears. "We raised you to be smarter and stronger than that. Did you even stop to think for a second about what you were doing? Debasing yourself like that for some *boy*? I don't even know who you are anymore. This isn't something *my* daughter would do."

I could have screamed back at her, asking where she and Dad had been the past few months and why they hadn't ever asked if I was dating someone, or if they could meet Blake, or anything else about my life other than details about grades and application fodder.

But by that point, I didn't really care enough to fight. I couldn't even muster up the will to feel anything but shame. Nothing could be worse than what had already happened, how I'd acted, what everyone had *seen*.

For two weeks, I did nothing but lie in bed and read

Harry Potter books, blocking out the rest of the world and living in as much denial as possible.

But I still heard that the story of my misfortune was picked up by a couple of Chicago news outlets. My name wasn't officially mentioned, of course, but there was no hiding. Every kid in school, every parent, every teacher, everyone I knew in the whole world was aware that the sexter who'd taken a golf club to her boyfriend's car was me. A simple Google search connected my name to the photos and the YouTube clip of me bashing in Blake's windshield. The story spread throughout the Internet and onto the cruelest websites as the newest unfortunate thing to point at and laugh at.

My first day back at school after the suspension was the worst day of my life.

THREE

So, I had been lonely for a long time when I found them.

It was about a month after the incident with Blake and the webcam pictures. Which made it about a month since I'd become the social pariah of my school. And a month since my parents had found out about the pictures and grounded me until the end of time or the end of the school year, whichever came first.

Not that being grounded mattered. I had no friends and nowhere to go. It was a moot point.

I'd been hanging out by myself a lot, is what I'm trying to say. Which had led to lots of quality alone time with the Internet.

I'm not sure of the exact path of clicks I took to find the first website. It was probably a link from one of the snarky forums I'd started to frequent ... the kind of sites that find funny or ridiculous or tragic things to make fun of in the vast wilds of the Internet. And as everyone knows, there are infinite amounts of funny and ridiculous and tragic things on the Internet. Forums that made fun of other people helped me feel better about my own stupid situation. At least I wasn't a weird kid posting fan videos about Justin Bieber or a baby kissing a pig or some dude getting blown into the side of a barn during a tornado.

There were more humiliating and painful things out there than what had happened to me. Not many, but a few. And for a while it was my personal quest to find the worst of them.

So I clicked on some link on some random forum post titled *The most effed-up crazies on the Internets*, expecting to be briefly entertained by someone else's idiocy or misfortune.

Instead, I was transported to another world.

A world with a pale pink background, a flowery border, a precious banner image of an Edwardian girl reading while kittens cavorted at her feet. And the dulcet strains of religious hymns emanating from an automatic media player to make the experience complete.

Somehow, I immediately knew I'd found my new obsession.

The blogs of fundamentalist Christian homeschooled teenage girls. I couldn't look away.

. . .

There were so many more of them online then I would

have expected. On that first night, I clicked around for hours, following webs of links and follower lists and commenter names and getting lost in endless pastel websites and Bible verses.

Some of the girls were genuinely terrible writers and unreliable updaters, but I quickly zeroed in on the queen bees of this particular blogger community. They were the ones who wrote daily, posted the prettiest pictures, and got the most adoring comments. And though most of them wrote in a sticky-sweet and florid style that often made me roll my eyes, they weren't afraid to be blunt about their lives and beliefs.

Slowly I began to understand what I was looking at—a culture that was so different from my own that these girls were barely on the same planet as me, let alone speaking the same language.

My first thought was that I didn't understand how they were possibly allowed to be online. Didn't their watchful parents worry about what their precious, innocent daughters saw? Sometimes I thought that *I* shouldn't even be allowed to look at some of the things I found online, and I was a jaded old Internet veteran.

But as I read back through archives, I found them talking cheerfully about how their Internet usage was fastidiously tracked by their vigilant parents. And the girls themselves talked of being ultra-careful to not go to sites that might "defraud" them or force them to consider sinful acts or make them anything less than pure white vessels of virgin holiness. They quite happily policed themselves.

It was so … weird.

My second thought was to wonder why the hell they were putting their lives out there for public consumption. Didn't they know about online privacy? Weren't they afraid of strangers reading? Didn't they look at their website stats and realize it wasn't just other nice devout girls who were reading their deep thoughts and looking at their personal pictures?

Then I realized that their blogs were a form of preaching. They *wanted* people like me to stumble upon them and read. They believed that sharing their lives and beliefs might help some random Internet strangers find the Truth. They were missionaries without even leaving the house.

Personally, I wasn't particularly looking for religious instruction, but that didn't stop me from taking their blogs on as my new pastime.

At first I just gawked like a slack-mouthed tourist, but it soon became something deeper. I wanted to do much more than just anonymously read. I wanted to participate.

. . .

"Dylan," my mom said at breakfast one day in February. "You're spending far too much time on that computer."

I stopped shoveling cereal into my mouth and reluctantly looked up from my laptop, where I was catching up on the early morning updates. Some of my favorite bloggers prided themselves on getting up at the butt-crack of dawn to milk the cow, read their daily Bible verses, make the family hot breakfast, and update their sites. They were hardcore like that.

"Oh really?" I said, giving Mom's ever-present work laptop a pointed glance.

"I'm working on a motion for the arbitration," she said, frowning.

I shrugged. "Well, *I'm* doing research for a school project."

My fourteen-year-old brother, Scottie, snorted into his graphic novel. I'd made the mistake of showing him some of the sites, and he thought the fact that I was fascinated with these girls made me certifiably crazy.

Mom squinted at me. "You haven't reinstalled that instant messenger thing, have you? Dad and I told you, that's off-limits."

I rolled my eyes. "No, Mom. God."

It's not as if I couldn't hide the programs if I wanted to. Mom and Dad liked to think they were badass electronics experts, but they hadn't been plugged into a computer for practically their whole lives like I'd been.

I didn't have anyone to talk to on instant messenger anyway.

"Okay, well," Mom said, going back to her own screen, parental duty accomplished. "Good."

Breakfast was basically the only time I saw Mom those days. As a lawyer for a big downtown Chicago firm, she was working on some endless insurance arbitration that had been going on since before my freshman year. Scottie and I had started referring to the case as her third child, which always made Mom laugh halfheartedly and then look depressed.

Mom usually took the morning shift with me and my brother, while Dad, a corporate partner in the same firm, was supposed to be home in time to have dinner with us every night.

As if Dad managed to make *that* happen more than once a week. And even when he was home, his bigwig clients were constantly calling and harassing him. He usually just stayed late at the office and rolled in around nine at night with bags under his eyes.

The one bright spot was that the previous year, Scottie and I had been deemed old enough not to have a nanny hanging around anymore. And at least my parents had given up on keeping me "scheduled" with lessons and sports teams and tutors. I mean, I knew I was lucky they could afford all that stuff, but it had been seriously exhausting to never have a moment to myself.

Now I had plenty of moments. An infinity of moments.

I went back to my cereal and my computer screen, and resumed clicking through my bookmarks.

I'd built up a solid list of blogs that I checked several times a day. Sometimes it felt like a part-time job to keep up with them all, even though I'd narrowed it down to a very particular group of girls with similar fascinating lifestyles. The ones who were the most wildly different from me.

I was really only interested in girls who were home-schooled. The more siblings they had, the more intrigued I was about their lives and how their families worked. And I gave epic bonus points for living on a farm in the country and posting pictures of farm animals. Especially cute baby farm animals.

In terms of actual religious beliefs, none of the bloggers I read seemed to be part of any particular Christian denomination, and they almost always belonged to congregations that met in people's homes instead of an actual church building. I did some research and found out that these churches were the most hardcore conservative and used the most literal, fire-and-brimstone interpretations of the Bible. They thought mainstream churches—with their youth groups and book clubs and Sunday schools, like the big Presbyterian one my ex-friend Amanda belonged to—were too soft and worldly. Home churches didn't fluff around.

I felt sure that my bloggers' families didn't exactly belong to a cult, since they were spread all over the country and only very loosely affiliated. But in some ways, it was pretty damn close to a cult. They were convinced they were right and that the rest of us were going straight to hell.

Something about that sort of complete and utter devotion sucked me right in and made me want to poke at it.

So, after reading non-stop for two months, I'd determined my favorite blogger—Abigail from *Abigail's Walk With The Lord*. Hers was the first site I checked in the morning and the last site I visited at night. She was clearly one of the most popular on the fundamentalist Christian homeschooled teenage girl blog circuit, and she got dozens of comments on every single one of her posts. Even if it was just something silly like a picture of her little sister with a cow.

Abigail was the third oldest out of ten kids, seventeen years old like me, and lived on a farm in southern Illinois. She was, of course, homeschooled and wrote cheerfully about her dream to get married soon and have as many children as the Lord saw fit to send, just like her mother and older sister. Abigail believed that becoming a wife and "furthering the vision" of her husband was the sole duty and purpose of a woman, and she wrote like she was perfectly content with her fate.

No, more than that. She wrote like she was blissed *out*. Like it was the best fate anyone could ever hope for.

No SAT's. No college. No career.

"Oh, ladies, it's the most blessed and spiritually fulfilling thing in the universe to know our appropriate biblical roles as women and future keepers of the home, isn't it?" Abigail would write. "I don't know about you girls, but I'm excited!"

And then twenty commentators would chime in that it totally was the best thing ever.

The weirdness didn't stop there. Abigail was considered something of an expert at being a Virtuous Maiden and girls had started to write to her with their burning questions, which Abigail posted and answered (with the permission of her parents) like some sort of saintly Miss Manners. If she hadn't been a sheltered, homeschooled chick who lived in the sticks and rarely saw people outside of her own family and little church, she definitely would have been one of those high school girls that friends turn to as the group therapist.

I ate up every word she wrote like it was topped with whipped cream.

But I didn't understand. Given that these girls were more or less kept under constant surveillance by their ultra-conservative parents, not allowed to go to regular school or hardly ever out in public, and barely permitted to so much as glance in the direction of an unrelated boy until they were involved in a parent-approved "courtship," at which point they were basically already engaged to be married ... in this culture without access to boys and flirting and dating and snide gossiping in high school halls, how could these girls possibly make mistakes and need advice?

But as I read further, I found I was wrong. Of course, the problems the sheltered readers wrote about to Abigail were sort of adorable, but it seemed there was still plenty to fret over even in this protected and seemingly clear-cut culture.

> Q: How can I be sure that my skirt is modest enough
>   for a church event?
>
> Q: I would like to have a feminine countenance that
>   pleases the Lord, but I don't want to defraud boys
>   or men. How much makeup should I wear?
>
> Q: How can I practice godly submission before I'm
>   married?

I'd gasped when I read that last one, shocked to see how they viewed gender roles in such black-and-white terms. We're talking, like, "yes, sir" submission. Men are the bosses and women are the helpers. There is a master and a servant, a leader and a follower. The world is that simple.

At the breakfast table, I glanced across at Mom, who was scowling at her screen and cussing under her breath. Attractive in a kicky middle-aged woman sort of way, Mom didn't take shit from anyone. Least of all Dad, if their occasional yelling matches in the basement were any indication. I knew exactly what she would say about this submission philosophy, and it would involve her manicured middle finger.

But even as I was vaguely grossed out by what my bloggers said, I was still fascinated by them. Every last thing about these girls was interesting. From the modest dressing to the gigantic families to the homeschooling to the fact that every single one of them had the same exact goal in life: to get married and have mini-busses full of children. No college or boyfriends or unfortunate incidences with webcam pictures. No choices or chances to screw up.

They were so different from me. And they were so … *happy.*

And finally, after two months of avid blog-stalking, I had actually worked up the courage to quit being a lurker. I'd posted a question on Abigail's site. My sad, pathetic query was,

> *Q: What do I do if I made a terrible mistake that I can't talk about and now I'm very lonely?*
>
> *Sincerely,*
> *Faith*

FOUR

My family is not religious. I'm pretty sure that neither side of my family has been religious for at least three generations.

As far as I can tell, the only thing my parents believe in is the doctrine of workaholism and the virtues of an occasional fancy vacation. My grandfathers both worship at the Church of Golf, First United Congregation of Florida. One grandma plays shuffleboard at a practically professional level and the other one painstakingly redecorates her house every six months.

Basically, no one in my family is interested in pondering the deeper questions of human existence. They like to amass all their possessions in peace, without thinking much about it or where they'll go when they're done. And I hadn't thought much about religion either, except as something other people did on Sundays instead of sleeping in, until I found Abigail.

Because, clearly, here was a very happy person who had something I did not have.

So that's why I chose the name "Faith" for my good girl *nom de plume*. It was as different from my own boyish name as possible, and it had a good ironic ring to it. As if *I* knew what the hell "faith" meant.

> *Dearest Faith* (Abigail posted on her site in mid-February, a week after I had submitted my question in the comments),
>
> *Don't despair! You know you'll never be lonely if you fully allow our Lord and Savior into your heart. Call to Him whenever you feel empty and He will fill you up to the brim with joy. Serve your beloved family, find ways to purpose to help even more than you already do in your home. Make yourself a dedicated tool of the Lord. Sit and pray on the Word and turn yourself entirely over to Him. I promise you that you'll never be lonely again!*
>
> *Blessings,*
> *Abigail*

After I got over the initial thrill of being publicly acknowledged, I laughed at her advice. Well, how easy! If reading the Bible and helping with housework was what it took, why hadn't I solved all my own problems long ago?

Perhaps because there wasn't a Bible in my house and our housekeeper, Mrs. Kowalski, got pissed off every time I tried to help clean up. Mrs. Kowalski was perpetually worried about getting downsized by my parents, and she had shooed me away from rinsing off dishes or trying to figure out the vacuum the few times I'd attempted it.

I stared at Abigail's response for a long time, excited to see my words on her page, but also aware that this was the point at which I *should* make the choice to let this go. I could decide that my odd obsession had gone on long enough, that it had reached a somewhat logical conclusion, and that it was time for me to stop being so ... weird.

Maybe I could find a new hobby, like knitting or walking dogs at the animal shelter or trying to somehow put back together the semblance of a normal social life. Or perhaps I could convince my parents to send me to boarding school far away, where I could start over and pray that no one would ever Google me.

But instead of any of those sane things, I found myself typing out a response in Abigail's comments section.

Dearest Abigail,

Thank you for your encouraging words. You blessed me greatly. I will purpose to call to our Lord and serve my family whenever I am lonely. You are so full of Godly counsel!

In His name,
Faith

I'd been reading these blogs for months and knew exactly how to word my reply to Abigail. It was a little scary how easily it came out of me.

. . .

After Abigail had posted my question and responded to it, unknowingly reinforcing my addiction, I fell face-first into my fundamentalist Christian homeschooled girl blog habit. I checked the sites like a drug addict looking for a fix, absorbing everything I could about their lives, pouring over pictures and links and Bible studies like it was my sole purpose on this planet.

It's not like I had anything else to do.

And being acknowledged by one of them made me want even more. I wanted to be part of things, not just an anonymous voyeur or random commentator. I wanted to be known to them. I wanted to go deeper and further.

And, in my mind, the logical way to achieve that was for me to set up my own blog.

Not as myself. Not as Dylan Mahoney, Known Slut and Psycho Window Smasher. What nice girl would ever want to read *her* blog?

But as Faith, my perfect alter ego.

Faith … Faith … *Faith*.

Faith had a lovely, wholesome life. She lived on a farm in southern Wisconsin with her three brothers and five sisters. Of course, Faith was homeschooled, loved to wear only dresses, and her favorite things to do were bake sourdough bread from scratch and study the Bible. Just like every other good fundamentalist girl, Faith fervently hoped that someday a godly man would ask her daddy if he could court and marry her.

I snickered as I wrote that.

"You girls don't know how good you have it," I muttered to my silent dark blue bedroom as I wrote my fake autobiography. After being chewed up and tossed aside by Blake, the idea of a genteel, parent-guided courtship was hilarious. And kind of weirdly appetizing.

Once I had Faith's blog set up, I decided that I needed a photo to really give it that personal touch. But not a stolen picture of some random stranger on the Internet. Everyone knows that trying to fake a photo online eventually leads to someone out there recognizing the ruse and exposing the lie. And this particular online world was small and insular—I had one shot to do this right. The picture had to actually be of me.

I searched through my closet for a while and realized I had nothing appropriate to wear for such a photo. These girls only wore demure, dowdy dresses and skirts, and everything I owned was too tight or dark-colored or modern. So I went to the thrift stores looking for outfits.

Even though I went alone, it was the most fun I'd had in months. I pretended Abigail was there with me, looking through the clothes and deciding which outfits were modest and proper. Together, we finally found one that worked.

. . .

"Wait, why am I doing this again?" Scottie asked, holding my digital camera.

We were in the family room after school one Tuesday in early March. I was sitting in an armchair, attired in my recently acquired bleached-denim jumper that any girl in my school would rather die than be seen wearing. My dark hair was in a long braid over my shoulder instead of in its usual careless ponytail. I'd added a touch of pale pink lip-gloss and subtracted the chipped blue polish from my fingernails. I was looking positively pure.

"Because I'm paying you ten bucks," I said to Scottie sweetly. "Now no more questions. Just take the picture, please."

"Man, you look weird," Scottie said, aiming the camera. "Like a brainwashed *Little House on the Prairie* freakshow."

I crossed my legs at the ankle and smiled angelically for the camera.

"That's the idea, little brother," I replied.

Once I had a suitable picture, I felt like I could really get into character. I began to write Faith's blog entries. First I created an introductory post, talking in detail about my fake family and my fake life and my fake beliefs. I filled out a back story, giving Faith a perfect rustic childhood.

It was weirdly exhilarating, and ten times better than any of the therapy sessions I'd suffered through immediately after the nastiness with Blake.

"I have the sweetest Mama and most amazing Daddy in the whole world!" I wrote, in my dark bedroom in my empty house. "They are the best examples of godly parents that I could have ever been blessed with."

Okay, the truth is, I did feel sort of squicked out by what I was doing at first. But as I wrote more, I convinced myself it was sort of like a creative writing project. Like for a class. It was educational! I was just making up a story about a girl and her life and posting it online. It wasn't my business if other people believed it was fact.

Right?

After I had a few entries posted, I linked to my site in comments I left on other blogs, and eventually the girls started coming to my page. By April, I had thirty or forty visitors a day. At least a quarter of them left supportive, chatty comments.

It made me laugh to think about how the rest of the visitors were probably big old voyeurs, like I had been, thinking that Faith was the real deal.

The morning I got the first comment from Abigail on my blog, I walked around in a happy daze. No one could ruin it. Not even the person who wrote *Dylan Mahoney = ugly skank ho* on my locker with a permanent marker, in handwriting that looked suspiciously like Blake's.

> *I absolutely adore your site!* Abigail wrote. *What an encouraging maiden of virtue you are for your sisters in Christ. I wish you lived closer so we could fellowship in person! Please keep it up!*

It sort of felt like being touched by a god.

. . .

A few days after Abigail commented on my blog, Amanda walked up as I was staring at my locker. The custodian had scrubbed at the words, but you could still see the faint outline of "skank ho."

"Hi? Dylan?" Amanda said softly, hugging her bag to her chest. "I just wanted to ask are … um … are you doing okay? With everything?"

I took a deep breath and looked at her, a hopeful lump forming in my throat. Amanda! She was talking to me for the first time in almost six months! Of her own free will!

For a moment, it felt like a reconciliation was possible. That maybe if both of us said the right words in the right order, we could go back to how things were before I screwed up. The world could be normal.

But then I saw Amanda throw an anxious glance over her shoulder, like she was afraid of who might be watching and judging, and my stomach twisted. She didn't actually want to be seen with me. I was still disgusting. I was still an exile.

"Whatever," I said, slamming my locker and turning to leave. "It's fine. You don't have to act like you care. Really."

I walked away slowly, waiting for Amanda to call me back. To say she did care and that she wasn't afraid of being my friend again, no matter what had happened or how much of a mess I'd made.

But Amanda didn't say anything, so I kept walking.

FIVE

ad, how come we never go to church?" I asked, over
pizza, on a rare Friday night when he was home in
time to eat. Dad, Scottie, and I were standing around the
kitchen island eating straight out of the box. Mom, of
course, was at work late.

"Huh?" Dad said, confused and only half listening, as
he loosened his Important Lawyer tie with a grimace.

"Did you ever go to church with Grandma and Grand-
dad?" I asked. "Like, when you were a kid?"

He squinted at me, his eyes tired. Dad's eyes were
almost always tired, unless he was contemplating baseball.

"Church? What's this about?"

I shrugged. "Just curious."

Scottie took a moment away from inhaling his slice of
thin crust. "It's because she's totally obsessed with—"

I reached over and clapped my hand over his mouth. "It's for an essay!" I said loudly. "For school."

Scottie spit some of his last bite of pizza against my hand.

"Gross!" I said, mashing the food back into his mouth and wiping my hand on his shirt. This provided sufficient distraction for Dad to forget about what Scottie had said, if he'd even registered it at all.

"Hey, hey, cut it out, guys," he said wearily, as Scottie pushed me and I pushed him back. I decided that later on, I'd have to bribe Scottie to keep quiet permanently.

After my brother and I had finished our customary shoving match, I brought the conversation back to the task at hand.

"Seriously, though, did you go to church? I'd really like to know," I said. "For the essay, I mean."

Dad shrugged. "Besides weddings and funerals, I guess I remember going once or twice, for Christmas or Easter, I think. But it was with my mom's parents or great-aunt or something. I think we just went to be polite. Well, you know your grandparents. They aren't exactly ... "

"Observant? Pious?" I supplied. "Faithful?"

Dad looked totally zoned out. "Whatever you want to call it."

Like I said, not too interested in pondering the deeper questions of human spirituality. Not even interested in talking about it for more than two sentences. Then something occurred to me.

"So ... are we not baptized?" I asked.

Dad shrugged again. "When you don't believe in those things, there isn't much point to all that ritual."

"Wow…" I frowned down at the pizza, a little scandalized. I knew what Abigail and her family would think about that. Baptism of some sort was the absolute bare minimum for being Saved. I didn't even qualify on an entry-level basis.

"Wait, if you're not baptized does it mean you're going to hell?" Scottie asked.

Dad sighed and ripped at the label on his beer bottle. It was obvious he would much rather retreat to his basement man-cave with the big-screen TV and prerecorded episodes of *SportsCenter* than have this or any conversation.

"I guess some people would believe that," Dad said. "Personally, I don't believe in hell. And I'm not sure what I even think of God. I put my faith in things I can see and touch and feel. I guess I'm fine with whatever gets you by in the world as long as you don't force your beliefs on others. I'm not going to tell someone else they're wrong to believe in a white-bearded old man in the sky watching our every move and keeping a tally sheet, but I certainly don't want anyone telling me that *I* have to believe in that in order to be a good person."

With that, he took a decisive gulp of his beer, looking a little embarrassed.

I blinked at him. This was just about the longest speech I'd ever heard my dad give on something other than the bullpen of the White Sox or the idiocy of clueless clients.

"Oh," I said. "Okay then."

"You guys are free to believe in whatever you want, of course…" he said, trailing off. "Just don't try and get me to donate money."

I wasn't sure if I was supposed to laugh at that or not, so I didn't.

We were all silent for a few awkward moments, then Dad's cell phone rang. He looked at the display and swore softly. "Hold tight, kids, I have to take this." He wandered off toward the living room, muttering, "One of the junior associates. Incompetent little twerp."

My brother and I glanced at each other, knowing Dad was done with the fatherly portion of the evening. Scottie grabbed another slice and headed toward his room. I sighed and picked at the pizza carcasses, half-listening to Dad bark into the phone at the poor associate who saw him more than I did.

. . .

Later on, I was in bed with my computer, working on a new Faith entry and trying not to obsess over how pathetic it was to be home on a Friday night, when Dad knocked on my door.

He peeked in. "Is everything okay, Pickle?"

I blinked at him in surprise.

Pickle used to be my parents' nickname for me (get it? Dylan, Dyl, dill pickle? Hilarious, right?) but Dad hadn't called me that in years. Even prior to the whole webcam picture thing, my relationship with Dad had taken a turn for the distant after I grew boobs and turned into a definitive girl. It hadn't helped when I'd quit my soccer league in eighth grade, which had been one of the only things he could ever be persuaded to leave work early for, and one of the few subjects we ever had to talk about. He'd transferred all of that sort of attention to Scottie.

And since the Blake Incident, he'd barely spoken to me at all. I guess that being called into the principal's office about topless pictures of your teenage kid being published on the Internet would be awkward for any father-daughter relationship. The phrase "excruciatingly humiliating for everyone involved and then never spoken of again" comes to mind.

I mean, Mom and I had gotten into plenty of shouting matches in the last few months, but Dad had more or less been treating me like we were casual acquaintances.

"Yeah, Dad, everything's fine," I lied. Because why bother changing the trend now?

He hesitated for a moment, his lawyer instincts no doubt catching that I was lying even though he was probably four microbrews into the night.

"You're sure?" he asked, putting one tentative foot in my room. "That talk about church and baptizing and stuff. I guess it threw me for a loop. It's just ... never anything I knew you were thinking about."

There have been a lot of things you've never known I was thinking about, I wanted to say.

"Just for a school essay," I said. "No big deal."

He'd stopped, one step into my room.

"How has it been meeting with that... uh, that doctor?" he asked.

After I'd gotten suspended, Mom had set me up with a fancy child psychiatrist to "talk about my acting-out issues." But after a few unhelpful sessions that were really mostly staring contests, I called up Dr. Brenner's office pretending to be my mom and cancelled the future appointments. No one from the office had followed up. And my parents, unsurprisingly, had forgotten about it. Until now.

"Okay," I said, looking at him steadily.

"Is school going well? Are your grades still okay?"

"Sure," I said. Having no social life had, in fact, done wonders for my work ethic. "They're fine."

"Because it's really important to keep them up in your junior year, you know. Colleges really want—"

"I know, Dad," I said, trying not to let my voice sound bitter. As if I hadn't had the college thing drilled into me since I was in elementary school. Keeping up appearances for the applications was the only thing that had ever seemed important.

"Okay, well..." he said. "If there's anything else you ever want to talk about..."

Ugh, save me from parents who intermittently want to pretend like they're all Involved.

While you're at it, save me from disappearing friends and hot boys who turn out to be awful human beings.

"Nope, nothing else," I said, with a small smile. "I guess I went through a rough time, but now it's fine."

"Okay," he said, turning to leave. He stopped and his shoulders slumped a little. "Hey, I know that we talked about going to that movie tomorrow, but it turns out—"

"You have to go into the office," I finished for him. "It's fine, Dad. The movie looked stupid anyway."

He looked at me with those same tired eyes, grimacing a little, seeming almost appreciative that I was letting him off the hook so easily. I couldn't understand why he did it. What was so awesome about being a lawyer anyway? When he was my age, did he dream of growing up and spending his Friday nights yelling into the phone at some underling while his kids grew up and kept secrets?

I knew one thing for sure—no way in hell was that *my* dream.

"You're positive it's okay?" he said.

"Yeah, seriously, don't worry about it."

I'll just hole up in my room and assume a fake personality, like always.

"Sorry, Pickle," he said, and closed the door.

SIX

My blog, *Faith's Surrender to His Bountiful Glory*, progressed nicely. So nicely that I had to remind myself every so often that it was totally fake and I was a big awful liar who was making it all up out of nothing.

But it was just so ... addictive. I researched country life and spun stories about Faith's daily chores. I looked up recipes and pretended to try them out. I did some further reading into fundamentalist beliefs and discussed fake sermons that my fake pastor had given and how they had encouraged me. I named all of Faith's siblings and created personalities and anecdotes for each one of them in a detailed spreadsheet, just to keep it all straight.

By the last month of the school year, I was averaging over a hundred hits a day and had a nice cadre of loyal commenters.

Your journey is so convicting, girlie! It is
AWESOME to see the Lord work in your life!
—Hisdaughter29

I wish I had half the energy you seem to have...
what a wonderful stay-at-home daughter you are.
—BlessedMaiden4Him

I got so much reinforcement from my readers that it was easy to stay motivated. More than that, it was straight-up *fun* to invent Faith's life.

As I walked alone through the school halls between classes, I would think about what I'd write next. I'd type up drafts of blog posts while hiding in the library study carrel eating lunch. As I deleted taunting, anonymous messages from my school email account or erased nasty, non-anonymous messages from my Facebook inbox (which were still arriving regularly), I'd make up nicknames for Faith's new kittens. And when balls of paper were thrown at my head during study hall and everyone snickered, I hardly noticed because I was brainstorming about what adorable antics Faith's younger siblings could be getting into.

And when I wasn't faking Faith, I was surfing the other blogs for ideas. I didn't plagiarize or anything, but it was easier to get into character when I was drowning in the language and beliefs and images of these girls and their families.

Sometimes I would stare at the family pictures they posted, mentally placing myself into the background, perhaps holding one of the younger kids in my arms, smiling beatifically.

Abigail remained my constant favorite.

There was just something about her—the complete confidence she had in her beliefs and her goals, the sweet way she wrote about her parents and family, as if they all completely adored each other and never disagreed or fought, and the recipes for old-fashioned food like soda bread and sticky toffee pudding that she posted with lovely pictures that got scads of fawning comments. Many more comments than I ever got.

Combine that with her apparent complete unawareness of the outside world, and her innocence was beautiful and somehow … contagious.

When kids around me in school would swear, I found myself flinching over how offended Abigail would be to hear such profanity. When I watched movies at home, I started averting my eyes during violent or sexy parts, envisioning how disappointed Abigail would be to know I'd allowed myself to see such unwholesome things.

To be honest, my obsession with her was only slightly based in jealousy. Mostly it was plain adoration.

. . .

"Mom, is it okay if I bake this weekend?" I asked one morning. I was, as always, on my computer and she was shuffling through a file of papers at the breakfast table. A cold piece of toast with one missing bite sat at her elbow.

She didn't even pause in her work. "Sure, Dylan, just don't burn the house down."

"Okay," I said, happily going back to clicking through all the recipes that Abigail had posted on her site. I hadn't decided which one I was going to attempt yet. They were all so tempting. Lemon cake or apple strudel, perhaps? Or maybe strawberry rhubarb crisp!

A full five minutes later, my mom jerked up her head.

"Wait, what?" she said, as if suddenly processing what I'd said.

I looked at her.

"Did you just say something about baking?" she asked.

I nodded.

"Like ... some of that pre-made chocolate chip cookie dough, like we did when you were little?"

That had been the extent of my activities in the kitchen with my mom. Half the time the cookies had turned out burnt. She used to barely be able to slice up oranges for my soccer team without cutting herself. She always made Dad do it.

"No, Mom," I said, rolling my eyes. "That cookie dough stuff is for wusses. I want to make this."

I turned my computer toward her and showed her a picture of Abigail's strawberry rhubarb crisp. It was perfectly browned and you could just about smell the sweet waves of baked goodness coming off the computer screen.

Mom squinted hard at the picture. "You really want to make *that*?"

"Sure, why not?"

Mom looked back at me, wrinkles of concern on her forehead.

"Don't you think that's a little … well, ambitious, Dylan?"

My first instinct was to snark at her—*and what would you know about ambitious baking, Mom?* But I swallowed back my sarcasm and smiled instead. I really didn't feel like fighting with her this morning. I just wanted to bake.

"Nothing ventured, nothing gained," I said cheerfully. It sounded like something Abigail would say.

"But … " Mom looked at the screen again. "Baking? That? Really?"

I could almost hear her brain churning, wondering what confusing new phase of adolescent development I was going through now, and if this one would involve a potential lawsuit or suspension from school. I just hoped it wouldn't make her remember the psychiatrist.

"So? I don't get what's the big deal," I said.

"I just … think … well, maybe you need to get out of the house more."

"You're the one who grounded me for forever," I pointed out, becoming more annoyed. "And what's wrong with baking? It's a good skill to have. It's pretty much the most wholesome thing I could be doing with my time."

"Nothing is *wrong* with it, exactly," she said, rubbing her temples as if she were in pain. "It's just very … domestic."

"So?"

"And I'm not … you know … I'm not the most domestic woman around." I had rarely seen my mom stumble so much for words. She was usually in complete control of all situations.

"No, *really*?" I said.

She frowned at me. "I just … where is this coming from? Why this sudden fascination?"

"Why do I have to be exactly like you?" I asked, ignoring her question. "What if I want to be different?"

She blinked at me for a moment, looking stung, and then shrugged. "Well, of course you don't have to be exactly like me, but—"

"Look, Mom, me wanting to bake isn't a judgment of you or anything," I interrupted, working hard not to let myself get snippety. I was trying to act how I imagined Abigail would act in this situation, calm and sweet and wanting to please. "I just want to try it, is all. I mean, something a little more advanced than pre-made cookie dough cookies. I think it'll be fun."

She still looked disturbed, tapping her fingers on the table. "Are you doing okay, Dylan?"

"Sure," I said, with a quiet sigh.

Mom reached across the table and put her hand over mine. "I know you've had a tough couple of months, sweetie," she said. "I'm … well … "

"What?" I asked.

She appeared to gather herself, like she was preparing to say something important.

"I'm sorry," she said. "Sorry that things have been so hard for you. And that we have such a tough time talking about it without fighting. It's something we need to work on, that I really *want* to work on, but I'm just trying to get through this stage of the case and then I'll be much more—"

"It's fine, Mom." I cut her off, gently disengaging my hand from hers. "This doesn't need to turn into a huge thing. I just want to bake, okay? It's really not a big deal."

We looked at each other and then she sighed, glancing down at her work on the table and then back at me.

"Well … all right then. Not sure what kind of baking supplies are in there … "

Before she could say anything more, I jumped up. "No worries, I'll walk to the store and buy what we don't have. I gotta get to school now. Bye, Mom."

I left her sitting at the kitchen table, staring blankly at the papers in front of her.

SEVEN

Abigail and I began to email back and forth.

It started simply enough. I wrote to praise her strawberry rhubarb recipe, even though my inedible rendition of it had somehow turned out both soggy *and* burnt.

I'm so glad you like it! she replied. *I'm so happy that the Lord brought us together through our websites! What an amazing blessing. I'm sure I have much to learn from you, too.*

Oh Abigail, you don't even know, I thought.

I wrote back to her after that, asking for a book recommendation, and she replied again, and pretty soon we were regular pen pals. Well, Faith and Abigail were regular pen pals. By this point, the situation had spiraled so far beyond that fateful day when I'd clicked on that first link that I sort of felt like an invisible bystander.

It was getting to be the last few days of school, which was wonderful (since it meant 100 percent lower odds of verbal abuse in the hallways and awkward avoidances of former friends) but also made me an anxious, fidgety mess. More than usual, that is. Being at school sucked, but if I didn't have it to go to every morning, I didn't know what reason I'd ever have to leave the house. I didn't know what reason I'd have to even get out of bed.

Scottie had sports camps and trips with friends planned for most of the summer, and, of course, Mom and Dad didn't work any less just because it got hot outside. We had a trip to visit grandparents planned for August, but that was it as far as scheduled activities with my family were concerned.

If I still had Kelsey or Amanda, or even Blake, that's where I'd be.

Instead, I was looking at spending a whole summer haunting my house solo, wandering the Internet and watching daytime TV in the cold basement, waiting for my family to come home just to have someone to talk to.

It felt like a death sentence.

I guess maybe a more normal, healthy girl might have put in applications for summer jobs. She might have called her relatives and asked to come visit or signed up for some classes. But I hadn't been normal for a while and none of that sounded remotely interesting. Besides, I was sure that wherever I went as Dylan, someone would know about what had happened and it would be terrible and humiliating.

There was only one thing that could get me excited

anymore, and slowly, an idea began to take shape in my brain. A ridiculous idea that had the potential to get me in huge amounts of trouble. But the more I thought about it, the better it started to sound, and soon I couldn't think of anything else.

I kept writing to Abigail—at this point, it was daily. We had quite a friendship … well, at least as much of a friendship as was possible when we'd never met and one of us was totally fake. We'd moved beyond just recipe sharing and pleasantries. She confided in me about worries involving her older sister and wanted my advice, and I asked her for her thoughts about some Bible verse I'd looked up online and didn't understand. We'd gently argued about which Jane Austen hero we'd most want to marry—(Abigail: Mr. Knightley; Me: Mr. Darcy, of course), and talked about what we wanted to name our future children. We'd send links to online videos of adorable kittens and convicting sermons and modest clothing stores back and forth.

Honestly, by that point, Abigail really was my best friend.

I don't know what I'd do without you, Faith! she wrote. *What an encouragement you are to me. I hope someday we can fellowship in person!*

So one evening, the night before my last final exam of my junior year, I wrote to Abigail about my ridiculous idea. An idea that I hoped wouldn't sound so ridiculous to her.

My father said it would be okay for me to go visiting this summer, I wrote. *He would like for me to be*

*exposed to other godly families so I can have more
experiences for when I am married and to help me
cultivate even more of a servant's heart. Do you have
any ideas about fellow stay-at-home daughters whom
I could visit? I know this might sound a little odd,
but it's my father's will, of course!*

I waited anxiously for a response, obsessively refreshing my email while I should have been studying for my French final. Had I gone too far outside the boundaries of what these girls thought was "normal" this time? Was inviting some strange girl off the Internet to come visit something Abigail would even consider? Would she get suspicious and see through me?

Her excited response came just a few hours later.

*Oh, Faith, the Lord sent me the best idea! Why
don't you come and stay with my family? I talked
it over with Daddy and Mama and they said it
would be fine. I've told them all about you for
months, of course, and they have always thought you
sounded like such a wonderful example of faithful
maidenhood! I think they believe you've been a good
influence on me.*

I literally laughed out loud at that. Me, the golf-club-wielding slutty screw-up, a good influence on the perfect angel Abigail?

Obviously not, but I wasn't about to tell her and give

up this ideal chance to witness her world. I didn't even think twice before writing back to accept the invitation.

. . .

After developing a detailed action plan and collecting the necessary materials, I was ready to go. First stop: parental permission. Strategy: divide and conquer.

Which wasn't all that hard, seeing as I hadn't witnessed Mom and Dad together in the same room for over two weeks. If I didn't know better, I'd start to wonder if they were the same person dressing up in different costumes.

But I managed to corner Mom in her usual place. At breakfast, while she was distracted.

"So, guess what, Mom? I found this cool all-girls camp in, um, Springfield that I want to go to this summer," I said, the very essence of nonchalant. "For two weeks in July. Is that okay?"

As per usual, she was barely able to tear herself away from legal briefs long enough to look at me. "Oh, really? What kind of camp?"

I put down a brochure that I'd swiped from the guidance counselor's office for some young women overachiever's camp in the capitol city of Illinois. The cover showed a diverse group of smiling girls doing wholesome, educational activities. The application deadline was long past and you actually had to be nominated by a teacher to go, but Mom didn't need to be aware of that. And I was gambling on the hope that she wouldn't look closely.

I rationalized that I'd be doing terribly wholesome things if I managed to pull this off and get to Abigail's house.

Mom glanced through the brochure. "This looks interesting, Dylan," she said, briefly smiling at me. "I'm glad you're taking some initiative. And it seems like a good place to stay out of trouble, too."

She was obviously referring to the lack of boys with whom I could get in trouble with.

"Thanks a lot for your vote of confidence, *Mom*," I said, irritated.

She gave me a withering look. "Don't start with me today, Dylan. I don't have time for attitude. Do you want to go to this camp or not?"

I sighed and slumped down in a chair.

"It would be good for college applications too, right?" I said. The magic words.

Mom looked down at the brochure, a tight expression on her face. It occurred to me then that she hadn't pestered me about college applications since before the Blake incident. But who could blame her? I'd screwed up pretty badly. She probably thought I was a lost cause, that there was no use in expecting anything out of me. My face burned in shame for a moment and I felt like crying, which hadn't happened for a while.

"Right, I'm sure it will be," she said after a pause.

I took a deep breath.

"So can I use the credit card for it?"

My parents had given me a credit card when I was a freshman, with strict rules about when and where I could use it. But I knew the credit limit on it was far greater than the stated camp tuition. I assumed my parents would probably check the bill, but I'd already planned for that.

Mom flipped through the brochure again, then put it down. "Well, I guess I don't see why not ... go ahead and ask Dad, too. His secretary said he should be home tonight."

I smiled, knowing I was almost home free.

Because, predictably, Dad had even less to say about my plan.

"Okay, sounds fine," he said without even looking at the brochure, sprawled in front of the TV with a glass of Scotch in one hand and his BlackBerry in the other. He glanced up at me. "Guess it might be nice for you to get out of town for a while, huh?"

I know they're my parents and that they're obligated to love me, but I think they were both relieved I wouldn't be around the entire summer, hanging out being weird and reminding them of how much they'd somehow messed up with me.

"Sure, Dad," I said. "Guess so."

From there on, my ruse was shockingly easy to pull off. The next day I used the credit card to pay the camp tuition money to a PayPal account I'd set up and blandly named *Summer Legislative Experience*. Of course, the account was tied to my bank account and the money was going directly back to me. But I wasn't going to use it for drugs and alcohol and designer clothes like other kids my age might, oh no! This money was going directly toward a Greyhound bus ticket and a wardrobe's worth of modest, fundamentalist homeschooled girl ensembles.

I was on my way.

I can hardly wait to fellowship with you! I wrote to Abigail. *This will be such a blessing!*

A month later, I was on the bus.

EIGHT

I didn't start to have second thoughts until I was one bus stop away from Abigail's town, and by then it was far too late to change my mind.

As I watched the flat green farmland of central Illinois pass outside the window, I felt some of the rosy-glassed denial I'd been working under begin to seep out of me. It finally hit my gut just what I had gotten myself into. And I started to realize that I was scared out of my mind.

Faking another entire person.

Sure, I'd acted in a few school plays before, which technically counts as pretending to be someone else. While I was with Blake, I'd pretended to be someone who was entirely comfortable with that sort of relationship, and after everything that happened, I'd pretended like the bullying didn't bother me. And I'd been writing in Faith's voice for months now, which had totally been all about taking on a character. I certainly had experience with faking it.

But none of those things really compared to two entire weeks of lying my ass off in person, twenty-four hours a day.

I smoothed my long denim skirt over my knees for the hundredth time. There was so much that could go wrong! I could say the wrong thing, or not know something that I was definitely supposed to know (or, on the other hand, know something that as an innocent homeschooled girl I was definitely NOT supposed to know), or look at someone wrong, or even blurt out something in my sleep!

"Oh, dear," I whispered to myself, practicing my fundamentalist-Christian-approved equivalent of an expletive. "Oh dear, oh dear."

In the headiness of my plan coming together, my excitement over actually meeting Abigail in person and seeing her life, I'd barely allowed myself to think about how hard it was going to be.

Every word out of my mouth. Every gesture. There was my entire pretend family I had to remember details about... there was a whole life that I'd made up that I had to keep straight. If I slipped even a little bit, the whole charade could come crashing down around me like a bad sit-com episode.

I'd definitely tried to think through every step of hiding my true identity. I'd buried my ID and credit card at the bottom of my suitcase, between layers of skirts. My phone was turned off and hidden in an inner pocket of my purse. I hadn't brought my laptop, which had felt painfully like leaving behind a piece of my brain, just in case some-one turned it on and saw something incriminating.

But there were still a million and a half other things that could go wrong.

And now I was stuck. The next exit was Greenplain, Illinois, where Abigail would be waiting for me at the bus stop. She knew what I looked like. I didn't have anywhere else to go. I was absolutely committed.

The minutes crept by. My heart rate crept up.

I reviewed everything I'd memorized about Abigail's family in order to calm myself down. There were her parents, who she called Mama and Daddy in her blog. There were seven younger siblings—four boys and three girls—who she referred to with adorable nicknames. There was an older sister, who had gotten married and lived some-where nearby. And there was one older brother, Asher, who tended to skulk in the back of photos, never looking directly at the camera.

There had always been something about Asher that intrigued me. Once, Abigail had alluded to "Asher's trou-bles" and asked us to pray for him. Which, of course, had the effect of making him even more interesting.

I couldn't believe I was finally going to see them all in person.

We exited the highway and began to pass through the middle of the small town, down an arrow-straight main street with Fourth of July buntings still hanging from the eaves. There wasn't much to Greenplain—a gas station, a hardware store, a dusty little restaurant with a few pickup trucks parked in front of it. It couldn't have been further from the bustling, paved city suburb I'd come from.

But I had seen so many pictures of the town on Abigail's blog that it felt strangely ... familiar. Plus, this was the sort of small town that Faith was from, too. This was the middle of rural America, where life was quieter and slower. And in certain places, much weirder.

The bus slowed to a squeaky stop in front of the post office.

"Greenplain," announced the bus driver. I was the only person who stood up to exit. It felt like everyone else in the bus who was awake was gawking at me, taking in my strange clothes. I would have stared at me, too.

I gathered my things and, heart booming in my throat, made my way down the narrow bus steps.

Was this really happening? What if it was some joke setup? What if she somehow found out who I was? What if she wasn't here? Could I just get back on the bus and pretend this had never happened?

But on the sidewalk, waiting for me with a huge smile on her face, was Abigail.

"Faith!" she squealed, skipping forward and grabbing my hands. "I'm so happy you're finally here! I prayed and prayed you'd have good weather for your trip! God is so *good*!"

My ex-friend Amanda may have talked only in question marks, but Abigail's favorite punctuation was clearly the exclamation point.

"Oh, wow, thank you for your prayers! They, um, worked!" I said, stumbling over my words, giddy. Hearing her say the things I'd only read on her blog was unreal, like stepping into a movie. I smiled at her, searching for any trace of suspicion, but there was none.

Abigail looked exactly like her pictures. Her long blond hair was pulled back into a low ponytail. Her face was wide and open and honest, with deep dimples at the corners of her mouth and pink cheeks from waiting in the sun. She was wearing an outfit I recognized from blog photos—a brown skirt and white cardigan that came down to her elbows, even though it was at least eighty-five degrees outside.

She seemed to be examining me the same way, still holding my hands. I couldn't even breathe. What if I'd missed some physical detail that would give me away? Or what if she could see the lies in my eyes? What if this ended right here and now before I even got two feet away from the bus?

The driver had deposited my suitcase next to me on the ground. I glanced at it for a moment and then looked back at Abigail. She was still staring at me, beaming.

"So..." I said. "Did, um, your dad drive you here?"

She blinked. "Oh, no. Daddy was busy with work, so my brother Asher drove me! You have to meet him!"

Uh oh.

From a shadow in the alley behind Abigail, a figure emerged. And there was Asher, the mysterious older brother, in the flesh.

"This is Faith!" Abigail told him excitedly, dropping my hands so she could hook her arm in his. She was bouncing a little on her toes. "Can you believe she's finally here? Asher can tell you, I've been waiting for this day for absolutely forever. It's all I've talked about for weeks!"

Asher cleared his throat and nodded his head.

"Very pleased to meet you, Faith," he said in a deep voice.

I'd instantly clammed up as soon as I caught sight of him. Asher was entirely too good-looking for me to feel comfortable.

Trying not to stare, I took in his light brown hair, which was a little long and curly on top, and a square-jawed face with startling blue eyes. His respectable blue button-down shirt was rolled up to his elbows, exposing strong brown forearms. From what I could tell, beneath his clothes was the body of a Greek statue.

It wasn't the sort of hotness that asshole Blake had. Not a preened and self-aware handsomeness, with muscles mostly acquired at a ritzy, air-conditioned athletic club and a lazy tan from trips to Florida or lying out by the family pool. I could tell this boy came by his appearance honestly, through hard manual labor and working in the sun. Asher had clearly earned it.

But he still scared me.

Because what caught me so off guard was the realiza-tion that I hadn't actually been attracted to anyone since Blake. Of course, I hadn't had much of an opportunity to be around guys who weren't harassing me or actively ignor-ing me because of my bad, Blake-created reputation. Even the so-called "nice guys" who I'd been friends with since elementary school averted their eyes and laughed along at the nasty jokes the bullies made about me. None of them had stuck up for me.

Guys in general felt dangerous and unknown. I'd more or less shut that part of my brain down and convinced myself it would be fine to never kiss another person until college.

But suddenly, with *this* cute boy, I couldn't help but notice how there was something about his face and voice, and the softness around his eyes, that sort of woke me up again. It was weird and upsetting. I didn't want to feel that way. I didn't want someone to have that sort of power over me again.

Because the last time I let that happen, naked pictures of me ended up on the Internet.

Asher was smiling shyly at me, waiting for a response.

"Faith? Are you all right?" Abigail asked, looking concerned.

"Hello, Asher. Lovely to meet you," I said quickly, keeping any coyness in my voice to an absolute minimum, conscious of the fact that I wasn't supposed to be noticing him as anything other than my friend's older brother.

In this world, flirting was looked down upon and considered defrauding. Faith would be horrified by the idea. In fact, *Dylan* was a bit horrified by the idea as well.

I already knew Asher had the potential to be a big problem.

∩I∩E

We drove back to their farm in the dusty family pickup truck. Abigail took the middle seat and talked excitedly without pause for the whole trip. Asher drove silently, leaning his forearm out the window, tapping along to an unheard tune on the steering wheel.

I wondered what the song was.

No, Dylan! I admonished myself. *Stop this right now. You are not here to get inexplicable crushes on completely unattainable boys! You are here to...*

What? What exactly was I here in this absurd situation to do?

"And I thought we could be in charge of dinner one night!" Abigail was saying. "You said you make a mean fried chicken on your blog, didn't you? And maybe you could make that red velvet cake that you posted pictures of! And I'm sure Mama would let us do some of the homeschooling for the little ones. They're excited to have a new teacher for a change! And we're hosting a Ladies' Bible Study Luncheon in a few days, and you'll be the guest of honor, if that's okay with you!"

I looked over at her, trying not to let my face quaver at the gauntlet of highly failable tests laid out before me. "That sounds wonderful, Abigail! Whatever you have planned is fine. I don't want to be any trouble."

She grinned at me, scrunching up her nose. "Oh, how could you be any trouble, Faith? You're a blessing!"

I smiled back at her, feeling a strange twist in my chest. No one had ever said something like that to me that I could remember. Certainly not recently.

We pulled into the long gravel driveway of the farm, and Abigail pointed out where they set up their road stand when they had extra produce to sell. We drove through a few acres of fenced grazing land, scenically dotted by grazing cows and sheep. Abigail recited their names and told me which animal belonged to which of her siblings.

"You can help me take care of my cow, Maybelle, while you're here! We can get up in the morning together!" she said, bouncing a little in her seat. "Just so you feel like part of the family! Oh, how fun!"

Just as I started to panic about the possibility of having to act like I knew how to milk a cow, Asher snorted. It was the first noise he'd made the whole trip.

"What?" said Abigail, looking at him. "Did I say something wrong?"

"She's a … she's a *guest,* Abi," Asher said. "Do you really think she wants to worry about milking a cow?"

I couldn't have been more grateful to him.

Abigail looked embarrassed. "Sorry, Faith. If you don't want to, that's perfectly fine. I just thought that because you wanted to be part of things … "

I glanced at her with an encouraging smile. There was something about Abigail that made me dread disappointing her. She seemed so young and vulnerable, able to be tipped over with the wrong words or a harsh look.

"Can we maybe just see how it goes?" I asked. "First, I'd really love to just watch and see how you all manage things."

She brightened. "Of course! That's a great idea!"

We pulled around in front of the house, which was so ridiculously idyllic I almost gasped.

"Welcome to Shady Acres!" Abigail said. "Our home sweet home."

We got out of the truck and I tried not to gawk too openly. It was a lovely old farmhouse on a small hill, painted pristine white with black shutters. There was a wrap-around porch with a swing and Adirondack chairs, and a large grassy front yard. Beyond the house stood a bright red barn and some fenced-in pens, and I could see parts of a huge, lush garden. Cows mooed in the distance and a rooster crowed.

I thought that maybe I had arrived in some country heaven.

"Um, wow," I said quietly, forgetting myself. "Your house is so beautiful."

"Thanks!" Abigail said, beaming at me. "Daddy renovated it himself when I was just a baby. Isn't he talented?"

A girl holding a baby appeared in the doorway and looked at us, and a general clamor went up within the house. There was the sound of calling and running feet, and children spilled out onto the front porch in quick succession. Four tow-headed boys wearing crisp khakis and polo shirts and two girls in summery calico dresses, the older one holding the baby, crowded together and stared at me.

Again the feeling struck that I was on a movie set. Or on an alien planet.

Abigail hooked her arm in mine and dragged me up to the front steps to the porch.

"They dressed up for you. We don't get many new visitors," she whispered in my ear. "They might be even more excited than I am that you're here!"

"Oh ... well, that's nice," I said, fumbling for words as I looked at all their small faces. What the hell did I know about interacting with a bunch of little kids?

"Everyone, this is Faith," she announced. "You all be good and polite to her, and remember what we practice about joy."

"Joy?" I said.

Abigail gave me an odd look. "Children, remind our lovely guest what joy is," she said in a teacherish tone.

"Jesus first, others second, and yourself third," they recited dutifully.

Whoops, I should have known that. It was a common saying on the blogs.

"Of course, how nice!" I said. "Thank you for reminding me."

Abigail introduced all of the smaller kids in order of age. "This is Matthew and Jed and Luke and Martha and Joseph, and this little one is Mercy."

Abigail took the baby from the arms of the oldest girl, whom I knew from the blog was about fourteen years old. She looked like a mini-Abigail, with the same wispy hair and round face, her hands clasped in front of her.

"And this, of course, is one of my greatest earthly blessings, Chastity," Abigail said, propping Mercy on her hip and putting her free arm around Chastity's shoulder. "She's been so sweet and offered to give up her bed for you while you're here so you can stay in with me."

I smiled, feeling touched.

"Thank you," I said. "That was very sweet of you."

"Hello Faith, I've heard so much about you," Chastity said, a little too cheerily. "We're going to have such fun with you here!"

Asher walked by us toward the front door, carrying my suitcase. As he closed the screen door behind him, he shot me a smile that I pretended not to notice, even as it sent a thrill through me.

Stop. Stop that immediately, Dylan!

"I hope so!" I replied, looking back at Chastity.

"Will you keep watching the littles for a while?" Abigail asked her sister. "I need to show Faith around the house."

Chastity's smile clouded over.

"But, I wanted to—"

"Please, dear," said Abigail firmly. "Be a good helper."

I watched Chastity's face as an obvious internal debate raged inside her. She clearly wanted to pout and complain about being left behind, as I knew from experience that younger siblings often did. But within a few seconds, Chastity mastered herself. Her expression cleared and she smiled and nodded at her sister.

It was kind of amazing to witness.

"Of course, whatever you say," Chastity said, taking the baby back from Abigail and going back inside, calling to the kids.

"Sorry about that. Chastity's going through a bit of a willful phase," Abigail said, looking embarrassed, as if Chastity had just thrown a screaming tantrum. "Plus, she's a little clingy and never has to share me, so I think she's a bit envious that you're here."

"Oh!" I said. "That's perfectly okay. I understand."

Abigail took my hand and grinned at me.

"Come up to my room. I want to show you my hope chest! I just embroidered a darling new set of sheets!"

. . .

Later that evening, as I sat at the dinner table and let myself get lost in the flow of words, my reasons for coming felt more valid.

Every member of the family was present, from Abigail's mom and dad bookending the long table, to Asher and Chastity on down to Mercy in her high chair, eating a home-cooked meal of beef stew and biscuits. There had been a long prayer, and now everyone was respectfully listening as each family member talked about something nice that had happened that day.

"They're putting on a little show for you, you know," Abigail whispered, grinning.

"It's wonderful," I replied, genuinely.

"I helped process chickens with Asher," said Matthew, the oldest of the little boys. "I learned a lot and it was real neat."

Asher, who was sitting next to him, reached over and ruffled his little brother's hair affectionately.

"Really neat," corrected Mrs. Dean gently. She was a kind-faced woman who looked like the absolute cliché of a mother with many children. When I'd first met Mrs. Dean in the kitchen that afternoon, she was wearing a pastel pink apron and had a smudge of flour on her cheek. She'd given me a warm hug that felt like snuggling with a pillow.

I couldn't help but compare her to my mom, who was all hard angles from her obsessive Pilates practice.

"Really neat," Matthew said obediently, glancing at his father, who grunted.

Mr. Dean was still an unknown entity to me. He owned a small house-building business, and when he came home from work, he'd greeted me politely, asked me a few questions about my trip, and then seemed to dismiss me. He had an outwardly jolly appearance, broad chested with an ample beard and ruddy skin. But there was something about his eyes that I couldn't quite read. There was a hard and watchful quality about them.

He caught me looking at him and I stared back at my food, my cheeks burning.

"Asher, your turn," Mr. Dean said.

Asher cleared his throat.

"I enjoyed teaching Matthew how to process chickens," he said, smiling at his little brother, who grinned back. I had a good idea about what processing chickens involved, and it wasn't something that required further details.

"A-A-And…" Asher seemed to be having trouble forming the words; his face looked anxious. Everyone was waiting patiently for him to continue, as if this occurred normally, and I realized that Asher must have a speech impediment.

"Spit it out, son!" Mr. Dean said, with a harsh laugh. The rest of the family stayed quiet.

I coughed to cover up my gasp at Mr. Dean's casual cruelty. No one else seemed surprised by it.

Asher closed his eyes and took a deep breath, and then he looked at me.

"A-And I was glad to help Abigail welcome her new friend, Faith," he said quickly. He blushed and gave me a small smile. Even though I didn't really want to, I couldn't help but smile back, charmed.

The table went even more still. Except for the youngest children, everyone stared at Asher and then at me. Mr. Dean was stern, giving a raised-eyebrow look to his wife. I glanced at Abigail, who pursed her lips and shook her head a little.

Something was very wrong. And very *weird*.

"Thank you," I said, to break the silence. "I'm very

thankful to be here with all of you. Thank you for your nice welcome."

At that moment, the baby burst out babbling and broke the tension, and everyone went slowly back to eating.

TEN

"Faith! Faith, wakey-wakey!"

I moaned and turned over to bury my head under the pillow. "Go 'way Scottie. Too early."

The voice laughed. "Scottie, who's that? You silly thing. Wake up! We have to go milk Maybelle."

I'd never been so instantly conscious in my entire life. I shoved the pillow off my head and looked up at Abigail leaning over me in the gloom of pre-dawn, smiling.

"Good morning, sleepy head!" she said brightly.

It all came back in a rush. The bus, meeting Abigail, Shady Acres, looking through Abigail's impressively extensive Hope Chest, dinner, the weirdness with Asher at the table, a whole hour in the living room of Mr. Dean droning on and on from the Bible as we sat around and listened quietly. And then up to Abigail's room, where I was given Chastity's bed. Chastity had been shipped off to sleep on the floor of the nursery, which she was obviously none too pleased about.

"Are you getting up or what? It's almost past six!" said Abigail, putting a hand on her hip. She was already washed and dressed, and I could hear the voices of people in the hall and downstairs.

"Six? Like in the morning?" I said, trying not to sound whiny. "Okay, okay. Yeah, I'm up."

I didn't even get up at six during the school year, let alone during the summer.

Slowly, I sat up and swung my feet around to the floor. I didn't feel remotely ready for the whole fish-out-of-water scene when I was this tired. All I wanted was to curl up in bed and sleep until a more reasonable hour.

"Rejoice, Faith!" Abigail said, leaving the room with a little skip. "For this is the day the Lord has made! See you downstairs."

"More like this is the morning Satan made," I muttered, looking down at the frilly pink nightgown Abigail had given me the night before so we could match. I made a face at it.

After yawning at least ten times, I put on my robe and headed for the bathroom. Where of course there was a line three kids long, patiently waiting their turn.

"Good morning, Faith!" the little kids chimed.

"G'morning," I mumbled, as cheerily as possible, stumbling back to Abigail's room.

After I'd put on some of my newly acquired modest clothes—a dark blue skirt that came down to my ankles and a loose summery shirt—and finally gotten my turn in the bathroom, I went downstairs.

Most of the family was already gathered around the table, eating big heaps of eggs and toast and bacon. Abigail and Mrs. Dean were wearing their aprons and standing at the stove, cooking up a storm, while Chastity ferried plates of food to the table.

"Can I help?" I asked, but Mrs. Dean shooed me away with her spatula.

"You're a guest, dear, sit down!"

I took a place at the table and glanced around. Asher looked up from his plate and I immediately looked back down, pretending to be examining the toast in front of me.

Breakfast was a much less formal affair than dinner, and everyone was talking over each other about their plans for the coming day. Mr. Dean was giving Asher instructions about mending a fence. The little kids were talking loudly about little kid stuff, and over by the stove, Mrs. Dean had her arm around Abigail and they were both laughing.

I slowly ate my eggs, waking up and trying not to stare.

Alien planet.

. . .

The first day felt both endless and quick as a flash. We traveled from one activity to the next without stopping for a breath, and I was very glad I had "guest" status and wasn't expected to contribute much.

All I really wanted to do was look around in disbelief and absorb.

After breakfast, there were the farm chores (where I watched with wide eyes as Abigail expertly milked her ornery brown cow in under ten minutes). And after washing up from chores, there was homeschooling for all the younger kids. Abigail worked with Martha and Joseph, quizzing them on the letters of the alphabet, while her mother had the older kids read out loud to each other as she bounced Mercy on her lap.

Apparently Abigail's own education was considered finished at this point, which I found strangely sad.

I helped Abigail make sandwiches for lunch, and then helped pick up after the meal. The food preparation and cleanup for a family that size was basically endless. Plus there were no frozen TV dinners, no cereal from a box, no ordering pizza. The Deans baked their own bread, grew their own vegetables, milked their cows, and collected their own eggs from the chickens outside. Everything was labor intensive and made from scratch. And delicious.

My mom's head would have exploded all over the neatly decorated walls.

The older boys were sent out to help Asher for a few hours that afternoon, and there was a whole list of cleaning chores that had to be done inside the house for the girls. Mrs. Dean had a giant binder of all the children's activities, and their time was carefully regimented in color-coded spreadsheets. I paged through it in wonder as Abigail swept and mopped the kitchen. She wouldn't let me help.

"It's time for afternoon scripture study!" Mrs. Dean said an hour later after looking at her watch. Chastity went to call the boys in and the whole family gathered around the table and listened quietly as Mrs. Dean read out of her pink-leather-covered Bible.

I longed to take a nap like baby Mercy, but I kept myself as alert-looking and pleasant as possible. Because if there was one thing that wasn't tolerated in the Dean family, it was an outwardly negative attitude. Everyone was sweet and compliant and good-natured a vast majority of the time. And anyone who acted up was taken aside and swiftly rebuked by Mrs. Dean, no matter how young or old.

Then more homeschooling, more farm chores, then getting dinner ready. It was always the women who cooked, of course. Chastity was still "in training," but Abigail and Mrs. Dean worked together like a well-oiled machine, getting everything prepped and cooked and on the table with the efficiency of professional chefs. I just tried to keep out of the way as they whirled around the kitchen.

In the half hour while dinner was cooking and everyone was busy with other things, Abigail beckoned me over to the little wood-paneled computer room off the kitchen.

"Come on, Faith, I have a surprise!" she said.

We sat down in front of her computer, a lumbering old PC my school would have junked years ago.

"I posted an ordinary update early this morning before you woke up, but now I'm going to tell everyone in blogland that you're here for a visit!"

I shifted uncomfortably in my seat. "Is that really a good idea? What if people … think it's strange?"

"Oh, you're silly! We're having such fun together, aren't we? They'll be happy for us." She nudged me with her elbow. "Let's take a picture."

A thrill of fear went through me. Except for the one picture I had Scottie take when I first started my blog, I hadn't posted any further photos of myself. And I was sure I had nowhere near the traffic that Abigail had. Thousands of people would see this post.

What if someone saw me and recognized my face?

Abigail took a digital camera from a drawer in the desk. "Say cheese!"

She put her arm around me and her face next to mine, and I tried to smile as normally as possible for the camera. We looked at the resulting picture, and I thought the fear in my eyes was a little too obvious. I looked tense and awkward next to the sweetly smiling Abigail.

"Um, sorry," I said. "I'm not very photogenic."

"Shush, you're lovely. Let's take some goofy ones, too!" she said, wiggling in her seat.

So we both stuck our tongues out and made stupid faces, and then loaded them into the computer and laughed at the results.

"Do you want to help me write my blog entry?" she asked.

I smiled, thinking how bizarre it was to be helping my online hero write her blog. I tried to imagine telling me-from-six-months-ago what lay in the future, and totally failed. I wouldn't have believed myself. Wouldn't have believed I'd ever have the guts to do this.

"Sure!"

We worked together for a while, typing out a scripted conversation about how we had "met" and what we were doing while I was visiting. I tried to help Abigail liven it up a little bit and include some tasteful jokes. As much as they fascinated me, I'd noticed that a lot of girls from these families rarely read anything other than the Bible, cookbooks, and Jane Austen novels, and their prose was often a little stilted and strangely formal as a result. Plus they used a lot of weird made-up words like "convicting" and thought that "purpose" was a verb. Abigail seemed to appreciate my help.

"You're so clever!" she said, giggling. "How did you get so clever?"

I just shrugged. "Oh, you know...a God-given talent, I suppose!"

"Mama will get such a kick out of this," Abigail said. "She reads it before I'm allowed to post it, of course."

"Of course," I said.

"Your parents read your blog posts before you publish them, right?" Abigail asked.

"Well...sure," I said awkwardly. For some reason, this lie hit me a little harder than all the others. If there was one thing my parents were completely oblivious about, it was my online activity. I could be running an illegal gambling operation for all they knew.

"I'm glad they keep such good watch on us, aren't you?"

Abigail said. "It's scary how big the Internet can be. I'm glad to just have my nice little corner where we found each other."

"Right," I agreed. "It is a pretty nice corner."

As Abigail was uploading a goofy picture of us to the blog post, she glanced at me.

"Faith, do you remember the first question you ever sent to me?"

Uh oh.

"Hmm, I don't know," I said. "It was such a long time ago."

"About the being-very-lonely thing," she prompted. "Because you did something wrong?"

I started playing with some paperclips on the desk, compulsively hooking them together and taking them apart. "Oh, yeah, I guess I remember that."

She put her hand on my hands, gently ending my fidgeting.

"Will you tell me what that was about?" she asked. "I mean, now that we're real-life friends."

Well, this was great. Time to come up with something tame and logical on the spot. I'd never really filled in this part of Faith's back story in my mind. I'd hoped that somehow Abigail had forgotten about it. What a total mistake.

"It's kind of a long story," I said, stalling for time. "And aren't we eating dinner soon?"

"We have a few minutes," she said, looking at me worriedly. "But … you know, it's perfectly okay if you don't want to talk about it."

I sighed. Her being so sweet and understanding made me feel even guiltier. I'd just have to wing it.

"Um ... so, I used to have these two friends. At ... church. And we were super close and did everything together for a long time ... "

"And what happened?"

"Well ... I started hanging out with ... another friend. Who they didn't like very much. They thought my new friend wasn't very, um, virtuous or faithful. So my old friends got really angry and yelled at me and then stopped talking to me."

Abigail's mouth was hanging open.

"They yelled at you? That's terrible!" she said.

And also not very fair. To my friends.

"Well, I mean ... I stopped speaking to them, too, I guess. Because I was mad at them for not trusting me. So it was sort of mutual."

"I see," she said, looking confused. "But ... what did you mean when you said you did something bad?"

I shrugged awkwardly.

"The thing is, they were totally right about the new friend and I should have listened to them," I admitted. "The new friend was ... not a kind person. At all. We aren't talking anymore either, which is definitely a good thing."

"But your old friends still don't want to be friends with you? Even after you realized you'd been wrong?"

"No," I said miserably. "But it's okay. I don't deserve it anyway."

"Faith!" Abigail admonished. "Of course you deserve it. Did you ask their forgiveness?"

I shook my head, folding and refolding a paperclip, not looking at her.

"Did … did you ask the Lord for forgiveness?" she asked softly.

"No," I said, suddenly feeling like I might cry.

"'If we confess our sins, He is faithful and just to forgive us our sins and to cleanse us from all unrighteousness,'" she quoted. "You know, from John. God knows that we all make mistakes, and we all deserve forgiveness if we own up to our failings and always strive to be better. Right?"

For once I felt like the flowery words actually spoke to me. Not that I was going to immediately call up my old friends and admit that I'd been wrong and they'd been right all along. But the concept of accepting that I wasn't perfect, and then asking for forgiveness, being cleansed, and moving on—instead of stewing around and then pretending it hadn't happened—was … something to think about.

Though in the more immediate sense, the guilt I felt about lying to Abigail was starting to grow and fester and become a heavy anvil hanging precariously over my head. She was so good and kind and believed all this stuff with her whole heart. And I was such a dirty liar who in no way should be here polluting her.

My mistakes were obviously not entirely in my past.

Abigail smiled at me and put her hand on my shoulder. She had absolutely no idea what was happening in my head, and that somehow made it worse.

"Come on, Faith, let's go set the table," she said, with a soft squeeze.

ELEVEN

I was avoiding eye contact with Asher as much as possible. Whenever he was around, I felt like a ball of exposed nerve endings, waiting for something to jump out and hurt me.

However, I found there was no way I could avoid watching him when he wasn't looking at me. And not just because he was total eye candy.

I couldn't help but notice how sweet and gentle he was with his younger siblings, and how he seemed to take his role as a big brother very seriously. Whenever he was around, he was forever giving piggyback rides or answering endless questions or quietly instructing. He would listen patiently to the little kids, not once laughing at them or shrugging them off.

It was undeniably adorable.

As Abigail and I did the dishes after dinner the next night, I decided to take a risk and ask about him.

"So what does Asher do all day? Does he have a job or something?"

Abigail shook her head. "He used to take classes at the community college in Carbondale. But that turned out to be a bad idea, so he works a lot with Daddy and around the farm. He's going into the house-building business with Daddy officially, as soon as he saves up enough money to invest."

"Why was community college a bad idea?" I asked, as casually as possible.

Abigail gave me a sidelong look, as if assessing me. I tried to look innocent, wondering if I'd taken my questioning too far.

"I mean, not that I—"

"Honestly, it's a little bit of a scandal," she whispered, interrupting me.

"Really?" Now this was interesting. Asher had a scandal, too? Was this the mysterious "trouble" that Abigail had asked her readers to pray about?

"You have to promise you'll never breathe a word to anyone about this! Not ever ever!"

I solemnly promised.

"Okay, I'm only telling you because I trust you completely." Abigail took a deep breath and leaned in toward me, speaking softly. "Last year, Asher met a girl from town in one of his classes and he claims that they *fell in love.*"

She said it like it was the worst, most shameful thing

that a nineteen-year-old guy could do. As if it were on par with throwing puppies in a river or running over a little old lady.

"Really?" I said, trying to look shocked. "In love?"

"Yes." Abigail went back to scrubbing a pan. "Daddy was so furious. This girl was a total stranger—she wasn't even a real Christian! She went to public school and goes to a Catholic Church. Can you imagine? Daddy told Asher that clearly the devil had gotten into him. That he had been tempted, and he'd been weak and had fallen, and now his soul is tainted."

"Wow," I said, blinking rapidly, trying to assemble all this information in my head. "You said he met her in one of his classes?"

"They were assigned to work on a project together, which Asher never even told us about, and they spent time alone." I knew that I was supposed to gasp in a horrified manner at this, so I did. Asher spending time alone with an unrelated and unmarried girl was highly forbidden, of course. It's as if everyone thought teenagers would start bonking like bunnies if they didn't have constant supervision. "And he told me that one thing just led to another and they talked about all sorts of things and he really liked her. Apparently, even though she wasn't a *real* Christian, she was actually very nice."

Imagine that.

"Well, what happened next?" I asked, wincing as I rinsed a pot in the scalding hot water.

"Asher snuck around with her for weeks, and then

Daddy found out. This was, oh, six months ago or so. One of the men from our church saw them together at a park. Holding hands and kissing, right out in public! Daddy got in such a rage, it was scary. He told Asher he had to quit school and come work for him, and that he wasn't to be trusted alone with any girl except his sisters until he was married."

"Oh my word!" I said.

She sighed. "Daddy said that none of his children would ever set foot in a government institution again, if that's the sort of thing that went on there. Asher was heart-broken. He said that he really cared about this girl, and she cared about him. But Daddy threatened to throw him out of the house if he ever spoke to her again. I mean, of course I understand why Daddy did that, but it was awful to see Asher take it so badly. "

Gross. It seemed so controlling and cruel. As if a nine-teen-year-old guy should be ashamed of being attracted to someone, and made to feel guilty for having a normal desire to hold hands and make out. And it was just unfair that jackasses like Blake were free to be awful to girls, while a guy like Asher, who seemed decent and kind (if disturb-ingly cute), was kept under lock and key.

The world needed more guys like Asher.

"Daddy was a little doubtful about you coming to visit," Abigail continued. "Because he still thinks the devil has a hold inside Asher. We all had a big talk about it, though, and I think you're even a bit of a test for him, to see if he can act appropriately around you."

So that's why he'd been so awkward around me. That's

why the whole family got weird and silent the night Asher said he was thankful for meeting me. They were afraid he was going to lose all control and try to defraud me or something.

Too bad I was coming to the uncomfortable realization that part of me wouldn't mind getting defrauded by Asher.

"How does Asher feel about all this? Does he ever talk about it?"

Abigail looked sad. "He really hates to talk about it, and I think he still feels awful. Daddy told him he'd visited sin upon the family. Asher is pretty sensitive, for a boy, and Daddy's always been on him about being a real man. Asher prays and tries to be upbeat, but I think he's still confused. It probably would have been better if he'd never gone to college at all and never even had those thoughts put in his head."

"Probably," I said, my thoughts spinning.

As much as I didn't want to admit it, Asher was becoming more fascinating by the moment.

. . .

Later that evening, I went up to Abigail's room and dug my cell phone out of my suitcase to call my mom. She probably didn't even remember that I told her I'd call to check in, but I didn't want her to try and get ahold of me and freak out because my phone was off.

"So, how is it?" she asked briskly. I could tell from the city sounds in the background that she was walking from her office to the train.

"It's fine," I said. "Lots of interesting people."

"It's just girls there, right? And they're keeping an eye on you all?"

"Yes, Mom," I said, half rolling my eyes. I almost wished I could tell her where I really was, but only if I could witness the look on her face.

"Well, good," she said. An ambulance went by her, wherever she was, and the siren was all I could hear for a few seconds.

"Anything else?" she asked. "The food is okay? You have everything you need?"

For a moment, my throat swelled and I almost burst into tears. I couldn't believe how much I missed my mom. And my dad and my brother and our house. My family was ridiculous and weird and all of us barely knew how to communicate our way out of a paper bag, but at least they were mine.

And no one there talked about the devil being inside anyone else. And no one expected me and my mom to cook and clean just because we were the women.

"Yes," I said, hoping she couldn't hear my voice break. "I do."

"Okay, Dylan," she said. I heard the call waiting beep. "Sorry, honey, there have been some big developments with the case and I have to take this. Call if anything comes up, okay? Stay out of trouble and I'll see you soon."

"Sure, Mom," I said, but she'd hung up before I could even say that I missed her.

TWELVE

My visit with Abigail settled into a pleasant sort of routine. Well, as pleasant as anything that involved getting up at six in the morning and wrangling a cow could be.

But it was refreshing not to be spending all my time on a computer or closed up inside. The little kids were all shockingly well behaved, but they were still a loud bunch, clattering through the house and slamming the screen doors. The windows were always open, and someone was always cooking or baking something, and there was always work to be done. Daily life was productive and busy and full of people.

I had to admit that all the Bible reading certainly got old. I could totally understand how Abigail was able to quote scripture by heart. At this point in her life, she'd probably been through the whole book twenty times.

Generally I blanked out while the reading was going

on. I tried to pay attention, but there just wasn't much of it that spoke to me.

The rest of their lifestyle was much more interesting, anyway.

The third afternoon I was there, I helped Abigail weed. We put on old-fashioned straw hats and carried little baskets out to the big garden behind the house. It was a huge plot of land, but impeccably organized. There were neat rows of tomatoes and squash and cucumbers and peppers and other plants I couldn't identify. And bright ripples of yellow and orange marigolds surrounded the whole thing.

I think Abigail had already come to realize that I wasn't as experienced as I'd claimed about gardening and household tasks, though she didn't comment on it or laugh at me or ask if I'd lied. She just patiently instructed me, praising my efforts.

"My sister does a lot of the gardening, so I'm a bit worthless at all this," I explained as I floundered with my little spade, face flushed. "I'm sorry."

"You're doing great!" she said, smiling.

I smiled back, wondering how one person could be so ... *nice.*

We worked side by side, pulling up sprouting weeds from around the squash. And I looked down at my filthy hands, dirt caked under my fingernails, and then up at the puffy clouds breezing across the blue sky. I smiled as I realized I'd never felt so comfortable and purposeful being outdoors in my whole life.

I caught Abigail watching me.

"What are you thinking about?" she asked.

"It's just so beautiful out here," I said. I wished I could tell her about the chaotic, traffic-ridden concrete suburb where I'd come from. How our yard was taken care of by a lawn service and that we'd never had a garden. How I'd never put my hands into the earth like this before, and the only vegetables I ever ate came on a salad at a restaurant or from the supermarket.

"'All things were made through Him, and without Him was not anything made that was made,'" Abigail quoted. Her face was so shining and earnest and open, for a moment I couldn't help but be desperately jealous. I wished that I could have such certainty about the world and how it worked.

I smiled at her. "You really love this stuff, don't you?"

"What stuff?"

"Gardening. Cooking. All these things that you … I mean, that *we* do all day."

She brushed her hands off and sat back on her heels. "I love being useful and productive," she told me. "And it makes life so much nicer if you take joy in your work rather than resent it. And this is what we're here to do, you know? As women. Feed the family, tend the hearth. We're training for the rest of our lives, doing all this."

"Right," I said. "But I was wondering … have you ever … oh, I don't know."

"What?"

I looked at her. "Sometimes I just think about maybe … wanting something more?"

She looked disturbed, squinting at me. "Want more than to fulfill my God-given role? No, of course not. Faith, there's nothing more to want!"

"Oh," I said, feeling embarrassed. That had been the wrong thing to say.

"Daddy preaches that's what's wrong with feminists. They confuse women by suggesting that there's something more they should want. Something more than following Christ's path. So they try and have a career, and then it's impossible for them to juggle having a husband and babies as well, and they just end up miserable and unfulfilled in all aspects of life. God and family should always be the priority. That's the way to true contentment."

"Right," I said, thinking of my mom. She didn't seem all that miserable. In fact, she was obsessed with her job and she was apparently damn good at it.

But there *was* also the fact that I barely saw her...

"Do you... disagree?" Abigail asked, looking concerned.

"No, not at all," I said hurriedly, and she smiled.

"Honestly, don't you just feel sorry for all those girls out in the world?" she asked. "Can you imagine not having a strong father to lead your family and a mother who takes care of the home? To flounder and have to figure it all out for yourself? To not have a peaceful, happy place to live and grow?"

I shrugged. I guess I should feel sorry for myself. "When you put it that way, it does sound kind of awful."

We went back to weeding and were silent for a few minutes. I tried to pretend that I really was Faith, that I really did agree that women belonged at home with a dozen babies and shouldn't want anything more than that. That all I needed to be fulfilled in life was to become a homemaker and a mother and a support to men.

But all it did was make me feel sick to my stomach.

"And don't you think there is something lovely about having your path laid out for you?" Abigail said, continuing as if we hadn't paused. "We don't need to worry about what we should do with our lives, the way that boys do, because we already know what we have to do. It's the most spiritually fulfilling and Christ-centered role a girl could possibly have. And it was given to us!"

"Of course," I said with a little laugh, like it was unfathomable I would ever disagree with her.

"I thank God everyday that he put me where I am and gave me the life he did," she said, sticking her trowel hard into the dirt for emphasis. "It's awesome."

I glanced over at Abigail. She had a smudge of dirt across her cheek, her clothes were unstylish and dowdy, and her hair was unfashionably long. She didn't know anything about current music or celebrities or how to apply eyeliner. She'd never kissed a boy or seen an R-rated movie. She would never get drunk at a party with her friends or dance around the living room of her own apartment.

Part of me wished nothing more than that I'd been born like her and had never known anything different.

Part of me wondered why it sounded like she was trying to convince herself that her path was so perfect.

. . .

Later that night, after we'd settled into bed, she said my name.

"Hmm?" I replied sleepily, only half-conscious.

"I was thinking about our conversation in the garden. Don't tell anyone this, but I've sometimes thought..." Abigail trailed off. And then, as if she'd found courage, she continued. "I've secretly always thought it would be really amazing to go out in the world and help other people."

I opened my eyes, trying to figure out what she was saying.

"Help them how?"

"Like...poor people. I mean, Daddy and Mama give money to families in our church who need it, or we make meals for a family if the mother is sick or just had a baby. But there are so many people out there, in cities and other countries. Who, you know, need help. So many children who are unloved and defenseless. And who haven't heard the Word of God. And who are hungry. Not just for Jesus but for actual food."

"That's true," I said, surprised she'd even considered this.

She sighed. "Sometimes I wonder who is supposed to help all the souls already on this earth. If we Christians just focus on our own families and the people in our church, who is going to help everyone else? If He were here, wouldn't Jesus be out there helping them? Don't you think?"

I stayed silent as I thought about what to say next. As

much as I wanted to burst out and tell Abigail that she could do or be anything in the world, that just wasn't what she believed to be true. She would be insulted. And Faith would never say something like that anyway.

"I've sometimes wondered if there should be any callings besides becoming a wife and mother," I said, thinking fast. "I mean, I know that's the best role, but there are godly women who never get married. Maybe that would be possible for you? Like, as a missionary? Or ... something else?"

Like a social worker or a teacher or a nurse or an international relief worker or a legal aid lawyer or one of the million other jobs that women, even devoutly religious women, were allowed to have these days!

"I'm a girl," she said, with resignation.

I stayed silent.

"But sometimes I wish that maybe ... oh, this is going to sound awful ... "

"What?"

She lowered her voice to the softest whisper. "Sometimes I wish God had more faith in me and I had been born a boy."

"I know what you mean," I said.

Then I lay there and thought of Asher, wondering if boys really had it much better around here.

THIRTEEN

Like most of the families I'd been reading about over the past months, the Deans didn't belong to a brick-and-mortar church.

Instead, they'd connected with other like-minded families in the area and formed their own little congregation. From what Abigail said, the families seemed to only socialize with each other. I didn't feel like I could ask directly, but it seemed as if Mr. Dean was basically the leader and preacher of the group. It was a very small and insular and protected community, like a large extended family who all believed exactly the same thing and thought outsiders were sadly misinformed and doomed to hell.

As Abigail liked to say, they thought of themselves as in the world, but not part of it.

So the next morning was a whirlwind of activity as we prepared to host the Ladies' Bible Study Luncheon. Eight female members of the Deans' small church were attending, along with some of their children. The Dean house was in a giddy frenzy.

"This will be such fun!" Abigail said as she tied her apron around her waist. "I always look forward to these studies. They are so encouraging, and this is such a lovely group of ladies. You'll adore them."

"I'm sure I will," I said, leaning against the counter and taking rapid sips of tea. I'd barely mastered feeling comfortable around the Dean family. The idea of a whole new crew of people scrutinizing my actions was freaking me right out.

So much could go wrong.

"And they'll adore you, of course, our guest of honor!" said Abigail.

I smiled as I watched her teach five-year-old Martha how to neatly frost the vanilla cupcakes. Martha was kneeling on a high stool, her small face scrunched in concentration, inexpertly wielding a butter knife.

"How's this, Abi?" she asked, holding up a surprisingly pretty cupcake.

"Excellent job, munchkin!" said Abigail, patting Martha's blond head.

The boys had all been banished outside, where Asher was keeping them occupied in the barn for the next few hours. Mrs. Dean had packed them up a picnic lunch. I glanced out the window, half hoping to catch a glimpse of Asher, but no one was in sight.

Abigail asked Chastity to take over Martha and the cupcakes, then looked at me.

"Come on, let's double-check the room," she said, linking her arm in mine and guiding me toward the living room. The furniture had been pushed back against the walls, and folding chairs and card tables were set up in the middle of the room. Mrs. Dean had spread white tablecloths on each one, and Abigail and I had collected bright flowers from the garden to put in little bud vases. A long table by the window was already half full of food.

"What do you think?" she asked me, looking anxious. "Is it nice enough?"

I realized she was even more stressed out about this than I was.

"Of course it's nice enough!" I said, bumping her gently with my hip. "It'll be the most elegant luncheon ever. Why are you so nervous?"

"Oh, I don't know," she said wistfully. "My sister Rachel used to do all these things when she was still at home. You know, decorating and preparations. She's so good at making things look lovely."

"And so are you!" I said.

"You're sweet." Abigail gave me a small smile. "But there's just so much to learn, you know? How to cook and clean and sew and decorate and teach and host. Sometimes I'm just overwhelmed with everything I need to know. And I worry that I won't be ... good at it."

"I'm sure you'll be good at it," I said with a shrug. "And you still have plenty of time to learn it all, right?"

Abigail was staring blankly at the room, chewing on her lower lip.

"Right, Abigail?" I repeated.

She blinked, and then looked at me. "Sure…lots of time, I guess," she said vaguely.

"What do you mean, you guess?" I asked, confused.

Instead of answering, she linked her arm in mine again and said, "Let's go get dressed! I have a surprise for you!"

. . .

Abigail's surprise turned out to be a Regency-style dress for me to wear. It was like something you'd see in a Jane Austen movie—a soft shade of yellow with an empire waist, small cap sleeves, and a delicate white ruffle around the modest neckline.

"You're a little bit shorter than me," Abigail said as she examined it on me. "But if I pin it a bit here, it should be fine. What do you think?"

I stared at myself in the mirror in her room. The dress was gorgeous. I'd never worn something so perfect. The dresses I'd bought at the mall for school dances in the past seemed cheap and gaudy in comparison.

"Abigail, it's lovely!" I said. "You really made this yourself?"

She smiled. "Yes."

"Wow, you're really an amazing seamstress." I swished around the room, enjoying how the fabric felt draped over me.

"I'm going to wear this one," she said, pulling a white dress with a dark pink sash out of her closet. It was so clean and pretty, I was drawn to it like a moth to the flame.

"Abigail!" I said, holding the white dress up so I could admire the detail of it. "Look at you! This is fabulous! You should, like, start a business or work as a costumer for movies or a theater or something. These are so awesome!"

She shrugged. "Oh, they're nothing. Just a silly little impractical hobby. I could never think to do anything else with them ... " She took her white dress back and looked embarrassed.

"Right, of course," I said, trying not to sound sad. I had said the wrong thing again.

. . .

As much as I was dreading it, the Ladies' Luncheon turned out to be very interesting.

The guests ranged in age from older teenagers up to late-middle-aged women. There wasn't a stitch of denim to be found in the whole group. Mrs. Dean had even dressed Mercy up in a frilly little dress and bonnet. Other guests had brought any small children they couldn't leave at home with older siblings, and babies were passed around and potluck dishes exclaimed over and recipes exchanged. Abigail introduced me to everyone, and they all smiled warmly and welcomed me without question. They'd all dressed up in similar old-fashioned outfits, even the older ladies.

The yellow dress really helped me get into character.

I simply pretended that I was performing a reenactment of *Pride and Prejudice* or something. I laughed demurely, said "how do you do" to each new lady, and sat with my legs crossed at the ankle, sipping my tea and nibbling on tiny sandwiches.

"We love to wear pretty things when we get together," Abigail explained to me. "Ah, isn't fellowshipping wonderful?"

I glanced around the room. Everyone was smiling and talking happily. The sun shone through the gauzy white curtains onto the plates of delicious-looking food, and the room smelled of summer flowers.

"It really is," I said genuinely. I'd never done anything like this at home. My parents had their couple-friends that they went to dinner with every few months, but Scottie and I were never invited. Mom and I had once made vague plans to join a mother-daughter book club a few years ago, but we'd never followed through. And with my parents not belonging to a church or volunteer group or political committee or any other sort of multigenerational organization, there'd never been a reason to socialize as a family.

Hanging out with women of all ages was honestly kind of nice. Until we got to the next part of the event.

After we ate lunch, Chastity was sent outside to babysit the kids who were mobile, and everyone sat and listened quietly as Mrs. Dean talked for a while about some Bible studies she'd done that past month which had spoken to her.

"Dear ladies, we must ask ourselves the question ... are we fully submitting to our husbands or fathers the way that our husbands or fathers submit themselves to the Lord? I would say this is something that we all stumble upon."

She looked around the room with raised eyebrows, as if daring someone to claim that they never stumbled.

"Can any one of us declare that we haven't once nagged our good, hardworking men? That we haven't felt a smidgen of doubt in our hearts about their leadership? That we have put aside being meek and mild and feminine, and instead believed that we, us weak women, knew better than our godly leaders? Ladies, we cannot listen to Satan whispering in our ears! To have a full, obedient heart for our amazing men is to have a full, obedient heart for the Lord. 'Behold the handmaid of the Lord; be it unto me according to thy word.' That is what we are told in Luke."

Around me, women were nodding their heads.

I looked down at the half-eaten vanilla cupcake on my plate, feeling a bit of it rise in my throat.

"Let's all go around and talk about a way in which we could be more obedient to these wonderful, visionary husbands," Mrs. Dean suggested. "And for you unmarried girls, speak of how you have stumbled on being submissive to your father, as he is a stand-in for your future husband."

Um, gross. I wondered what my dad would think if I told him what I was listening to. I'm sure he'd be as squicked out as I was.

I listened as they went around the circle in a weird sort of group therapy session, anxiety growing in the pit of my stomach about what I would report. One woman mentioned getting short-tempered with her husband when he tracked mud into the freshly cleaned kitchen. A girl about my age talked about how she had sassed back to her father when he asked her to do a chore, and how she had been rightly punished.

Another woman, who had a sleeping infant in her lap, spoke with tears in her eyes of how she had doubted her husband to his face about his ability to bring in money for the family.

"I'm so ashamed," she said, as the women closest to her patted her on the back and made soothing noises. "He says that God will provide and that it's my fault because I need to have more faith, but it's hard when he hasn't worked in weeks, and he spends all his time on the computer and won't tell me what he's doing on it, and there's hardly money for groceries." She took a deep, shuddering breath, and then smiled dimly. "But he's right, of course. God will come through for us. I'm sure it is my fault for doubting my dear husband."

Her fault. Right.

When the circle came around to me, I smiled to hide my discomfort and said that since I was just visiting, I didn't know what to say.

"Well, think of something from when you were with your family last week, dear," suggested Mrs. Dean with an encouraging smile. "I'm sure there was a time when you stumbled."

"Um," I said, my mind racing, and spoke without thinking it through. "Well... I suppose that, at times, I've wondered if I'm the daughter that my father wanted."

I looked around the room. There were a lot of confused, furrowed brows.

"And in my heart, I've wished that I could make him more proud. And that maybe he would...uh...be a bit more attentive. To me."

Abigail was giving me a sad look, like she couldn't feel more sorry for me.

"So what do you think the Lord would want you to do differently?" asked Mrs. Dean.

I cringed. "Be a better daughter, I guess?" I suggested.

She nodded encouragingly. "And perhaps you could reach out to him? Let him know that you need more direction from him. Not framed in a critical way, of course...no one likes a demanding, opinionated girl. But gently and lovingly ask for more guidance, because you value his leadership and his place in your life so much."

"Right," I said. "I suppose I could do that."

"I'm sure that he is proud of you, Faith," Mrs. Dean said. "Some men just don't remember to express it. Their minds are too wrapped up in other, more important matters. But sometimes we need to ask for what we need."

I couldn't argue with her there.

FOURTEEN

Things had gotten awkward with Asher.

There was just no other way to put it. Over the few days I'd been there, I'd caught him looking at me several times. Sometimes he would smile, sometimes it was as if he didn't see me, and other times he would look irritated and stormy, as if my presence bothered him.

The last one, at least, I was used to.

He rarely talked to me, except for obligatory things like "Excuse me" and "Please pass the salt."

I had no idea what to think about him, especially since Abigail had told me about his past. I wondered if he was still in love with that girl, or if he actually believed he'd acted wrongly.

I really couldn't accept that I'd come all this way just to crush on a confused fundamentalist Christian boy who would despise me if he knew who I really was—a crush that could lead to nothing but trouble and heartbreak. Perhaps even more trouble and heartbreak than Blake had rained down. Hadn't I learned anything at all?

Plus there was the fact that I didn't want him to get in trouble by interacting with me too much.

The safest thing to do was be as cold as possible and pretend he was just another face in the crowd, I decided. No matter how sweet and upsettingly attractive he was.

. . .

The day after the luncheon, Abigail and I were sent out to gather eggs from the chicken coop by the barn. I found this chore to be particularly traumatizing—sneaking through the straw and hunting for eggs felt like I was stealing from the mama chickens or something. And their beaks and jerky bird movements made me nervous.

I much preferred to get my eggs out of a carton. From the air-conditioned store.

So when Abigail was called inside to help her mom with something, I snuck over to the far side of the barn and stopped working. Though it smelled like manure and was littered with rusty old farm implements, at least I was hidden from the house. If anyone caught me I could say I was taking a break.

Though I didn't expect Asher to be the one to find me.

"Good haul today?" he asked, from right over my shoulder, scaring the hell out of me.

"Oh! Um, yeah!" I said brightly, holding out my basket so he could see the eight eggs inside.

As he looked into the basket and then smiled at me, I tried not to notice the way his sweaty gray T-shirt was glued to his chest or the way his hair damply stuck up in all directions. He'd obviously been working hard.

I found my mind drifting to wondering what it would feel like to have those arms around me, pulling me close ... *stop*.

"So, what have you been up to today?" I asked, trying to distract myself.

He shrugged, wiping his forehead with a red-and-white checked bandana he had in his pocket. It was adorable.

"This and that," he said. He leaned back against some bales of straw that were stacked behind the barn, letting himself slide down until he was crouched on the ground. "Dad's got me running all over today. I sometimes hide out back here, too."

"It's a good hiding spot," I said, sitting down beside him, the straw tickling my back as I crouched. "Sort of like its own little world."

As I sat down, I felt Asher go still next to me, like a startled woodland creature.

"Y-You know, I better go," he said quickly, glancing around, sounding almost in a panic. He moved to stand up.

"Why? Can't you take a break?" I asked, inwardly cringing as I hoped that didn't sound flirty.

"Well ... "

"Um, sorry. I'll just move down here," I said, getting

up and walking at least ten feet away to stand by some neglected gardening tools. "Is this okay?"

I grinned at him as I sat down again, and he smiled uncertainly back. I hoped he saw at least some of the absurdity of the situation, but I couldn't count on it. He was still a total mystery.

Though one thing was for sure—Asher was obviously a guy who was comfortable with silence. He sat there, not looking at me, until I couldn't resist breaking the calm.

"Abigail said you took some classes at a community college," I said.

Asher nodded, still not looking at me.

"How was it? I've always wondered."

He looked over at me and blinked. "About college?" he asked.

"Just curious. What sort of classes?"

Asher actually looked like he was on the verge of blushing, his tanned cheeks pink. "Various subjects," he said. "But computers, mostly."

"That's cool," I said.

He laughed morosely. "Well, it *was* cool. Past tense."

"Why did you stop?" I asked. I was curious to see if he would openly admit the truth.

"Dad decided there wasn't much point in it," Asher said, staring off across the back field. "And he's right. I'm just going into the building business with him, and there aren't really any computers to program while you're putting up a house."

"I guess," I said. It was the same sort of reasoning

Abigail had used. If your path was fixed, why bother learning what else was out there? In a way, it was easier. You'd never know regret.

"It—it—it's just, I've always been interested in computers, you know?" he said quickly, sounding a little ashamed. "Ever since we got one when I was a kid, I've been playing around with it, trying to figure out how it works, writing little programs and things. I built Abi's site, and other people have tried to hire me to build websites. But Dad doesn't think that's important work, because it's not actually building something physical, just messing around with 1's and 0's, as he says. And then with all the other stuff that happened … " He stopped.

"What other stuff?" I asked innocently.

"Oh, nothing you need to know about," he muttered.

"Try me," I said.

He gave me a doubtful look, knitting together his eyebrows.

Then he opened his mouth, as if he were about to talk, and closed it again. His lips were a thin, determined line. "No, i-i-it's shameful … nothing a nice girl like you needs to hear," he finally said.

Ha, nice. As if.

"But—" I said.

"I'm sure Abigail has told you some of it," he said, standing up. "She has trouble keeping quiet sometimes. But honestly, Faith, it's really best if you stay away from me. I'm damaged goods, and I'm not going to drag anyone else down with me. I swore I wouldn't."

"Asher, you wouldn't—"

He interrupted again, almost pleading with me. "Faith, p-please don't."

He shook his head and started to walk by me, on his way back toward the house. But he hesitated in front of me and looked down at my face. I looked up at him, at his sad and tormented eyes, and without thinking further I reached out and took ahold of his ankle, my hand clutching his dusty jeans.

I couldn't stop myself. All I wanted to do was touch him, comfort him, and somehow assure him that he wasn't an awful failure as a human. That just because he'd liked a girl who wasn't parent-approved, it didn't mean he was damaged.

And I wanted to tell him how I knew what he was going through—that I'd also made a mistake that had embarrassed my family and made me an outcast. And that I knew exactly what that sort of humiliated regret felt like.

But I couldn't say anything. I could only hold his ankle. Which was kind of a weird thing, I know, but it was all I could think of to do. I didn't even mean it in a seductive way, especially since the idea of that still freaked me out. I just wanted to connect with him somehow.

Asher's eyes went wide at my grasp. I squeezed gently, looking him straight in the eye, trying to communicate through my fingers that it was okay. That I understood and accepted him.

"You … you … you really shouldn't do that." His voice was husky. A bead of sweat trickled down his forehead and landed in the dirt next to my shoe.

"I know," I replied. "I'm sorry. I . . . can't really help it."

He made a strangled sort of sound and gently shook my hand off his leg.

"Please, Faith," he said. "Don't make my mistake. God is always watching."

And with that, he walked quickly away.

I hugged my knees up to my chest and watched him go, more confused than ever.

FIFTEEN

I was helping Abigail wash dishes after breakfast when her mom came up and put her arms around the two of us.

"Exciting news, girlie girls!" she whispered in a baby-talk voice. "Daddy just told me we're expecting special company for dinner."

I still wasn't used to how she referred to her own husband as "Daddy." Yuck.

But I smiled at her and carefully set the plate I was drying in the dish rack. "That's great!" I said.

Abigail was looking down at the soapy water, her eyes wide.

"Who's coming?" she asked.

"Well, Rachel and Elijah and the baby," said Mrs. Dean. Abigail's twenty-year-old sister had gotten married just over a year ago and had a two-month-old little boy.

"Along with Elijah's brother, Beau. You remember him, right, Abigail? Such a nice, godly young man."

I glanced at Abigail again, and it looked like she wasn't breathing.

"You'll just love to meet Elijah and Rachel," Mrs. Dean said to me, squeezing my shoulder. "Samuel is a darling baby, and Rachel is such a sweet little mama! Elijah just adores her. It's been such a blessing to see young people living out the example of a good, Biblical marriage."

As she chatted about the visitors, I kept shooting looks at Abigail. She'd started washing dishes again but was going much slower, her heart clearly not in it. Her face was tense and for once I could see the physical similarities between her and Asher.

"I'd just love it if they came over more often," Mrs. Dean said, nudging Abigail with her hip. "Wouldn't you like to see more of them, too? Especially when they bring a certain someone?"

Abigail dropped the glass she was holding and it shattered all over the sink.

"Goodness, Abigail!" snapped her mother, the coy-conspiratorial voice gone. "Don't be so careless! Clean that up!"

"Sorry, Mama," Abigail said, starting to pick up the pieces.

"Honestly," Mrs. Dean said as she flounced away toward the living room. "Sometimes you wouldn't know you're almost eighteen. Try not to cut yourself, for Heaven's sake."

I watched Mrs. Dean go, shocked at her sudden turn, then started to help Abigail pick up the glass out of the sink.

"Are you okay?" I asked softly.

"Oh, except for my clumsiness, I'm fine!" she said, with a suspicious sort of brightness.

"Are you sure? Because—"

"Ouch!" Abigail gasped, interrupting. A piece of glass had nicked her thumb. "Goodness, could I be any more stupid?"

"Abi, it was an accident." I noticed there were tears in her eyes, and I could tell they weren't related to the cut on her finger. "Okay, what's really going on?"

"It's nothing," she said, almost with a sob. "I shouldn't say anything at all about it."

"About what? Is it something about this brother who's coming?"

She looked at me, thumb in her mouth and her blue eyes huge and wet, and I was reminded of a scared little kid. Reluctantly, she nodded.

"What about him?" An uncomfortable suspicion was beginning to form in my brain, but I didn't want to jump to conclusions.

Abigail turned to face the sink again, examining her thumb. "It's silly."

"Clearly you're upset about something," I pointed out. "So it must not be silly. Come on, spit it out."

She turned and gave me a tremulous smile, putting her hand on my arm. "You're such a good friend, Faith. What would I do without you here?"

I laughed. "You'd probably be just fine. I mean, you saw how my oatmeal just turned out this morning."

She pulled away and wiped at her eyes, smiling. "Maybe that's why I'm all emotional."

"Will you tell me what's really wrong?"

Abigail sighed and drummed her fingers on the sink.

"I like Elijah, I really do," she said. "And his brother Beau seems like a ... like a nice man. He's been coming to our church for a bit and he owns his own business and everything. He works with Daddy sometimes, and Daddy thinks he's wonderful and keeps saying that Beau just needs to find a good girl and settle down."

"Oh, he's ... not married?" I asked, though I already knew the answer. Of course he wasn't. His attendance at this dinner had a definite purpose.

Abigail shook her head, biting her lip.

"Um ... how old is he?"

"Twenty-eight," she whispered.

I couldn't help it. I laughed. The idea was just too ridiculous. "And your parents just want you to—"

Abigail held up her hands to quiet me. "Shhh, Mama could be listening!"

"They honestly think that you and this Beau would be a good ... match?" I finished quietly, crossing my arms.

"He's a fine man," she said weakly. "Very Biblical. I could do much worse. Daddy and he have theological discussions all the time and they always agree on everything. You know how hard that is to find. Sometimes Daddy even has him speak on Sundays, which is a big deal because

Daddy doesn't give the podium to just anyone. And if Daddy likes him, then..."

She trailed off, the implication clear. If her father ordered it, Abigail would have to obey. And be married to her brother-in-law's brother, eleven years older than she was, whether she was excited about it or not.

I mean, I knew that some families still practiced this sort of half-arranged Biblical courtship—it was often proudly mentioned on the blogs I'd visited, especially when older siblings were married off. And in a way it made sense. If you barely let your daughters out of your sight, don't let them speak to any boys or hang out in mixed groups on their own, how are they supposed to find anyone to marry, let alone a guy who fits the exact religious specifications? If parents didn't go out looking for eligible bachelors for their daughters, their daughters would never be able to fulfill their appropriate roles as wives and helpmeets.

But the whole concept made me feel queasy.

I stared at Abigail, at a complete loss about what to say. "This is disgusting" or "they're crazy" or "let's haul ass out of here and run away to where people are living in the twenty-first century" were not things that would come out of Faith's mouth.

The most appropriate reaction would be for me to be delighted for Abigail. She was closing in on her destiny.

But why was she crying? Why did she look so upset about it?

Any lingering feelings I'd had that visiting the Deans was a fun game had faded away. This was Abigail's life, and she didn't get to leave it at the end of two weeks. I reached over and squeezed her arm.

She set her shoulders, took a deep breath, and smiled at me. Wide and brilliant and fake. "Let's figure out a menu. How fun!"

. . .

Beau was horrible.

He was good-looking enough, I guess, with military-short reddish hair and a fussily trimmed goatee. His brown polo shirt was carefully ironed and his khakis had a crisp crease. He cut his food neatly and complimented all the "ladies" on the cooking. He joked with the small kids, who stared at him with starry eyes.

But there was something…wrong. Some glossy sheen to him that made me feel like the whole package was a lie. Some leer to his eye as he looked at Abigail, even though he never talked directly to her. Some smarmy smugness around his mouth that turned my stomach.

It was obvious what his intentions were.

"With business going so well," he said to Mr. Dean as he patted his mouth with a napkin, "I'm thinking of buying a nice piece of property and building myself a house up the road a tick."

"Up the road from here?" asked Mrs. Dean. "Isn't that wonderful! Abigail, don't you think that's wonderful? That's so close!"

She beamed at Abigail, who smiled weakly and then looked down at her plate. "It sure is."

"And building a whole new house. That's just lovely!" said Rachel. She was sitting across from me, holding her baby boy who was, admittedly, adorable. Her face was glowing, and she and her husband had just announced that she was pregnant again.

Everyone had clapped and congratulated them, but when I'd glanced over at Abigail, I could tell that her joy was a little forced. She was concerned about her sister. When we'd been cooking earlier, Abigail had told me that Rachel's first pregnancy was tough and her doctor had told her to wait awhile before having another baby. Obviously, Rachel and Elijah hadn't taken his advice. Having more babies was more important.

"Well, it's about time," bellowed Mr. Dean at Beau, nodding. "You need to settle on down, young man, and have yourself some godly arrows. 'Blessed is the man whose quiver is full of them. They will not be put to shame when they contend with their enemies in the gate.' Psalm 127:3."

"Amen," said Elijah, putting his arm around his wife, who smiled adoringly at him.

"Amen," said Mrs. Dean.

"Amen," repeated the rest of the table. Except for me. I still hadn't gotten the hang of that.

Mr. Dean looked down the table at his family, the same sort of smug possessive look on his face that Beau had earlier. "A man isn't anything without a family. And a woman," he said as he looked pointedly at Abigail, "isn't anything without her man. Isn't that right, daughter?"

Abigail put her hands in her lap, and I could sense that she was bracing herself. "Of course, Daddy."

I glanced across the table at Asher, who was still refusing to meet my eye after our awkward interaction the day before. But he also looked worried and muddled, shooting glances at Abigail and at Beau and compulsively moving his food around his plate.

I wasn't the only one who was disturbed by the situation.

SIXTEEN

Later that night, after the guests were gone and everyone was in bed, I could hear Abigail quietly catching her breath. It sounded like she was trying to stop crying.

"Abigail?" I finally whispered, looking across the darkened room at her.

"Faith, you're still awake?" she replied, sniffling.

"Yeah ... are you okay?"

"Oh, it's silly," she said.

"What's silly?"

There was a long pause.

"Do you know if ... do your parents have anyone picked out for you?" she asked. "I mean, I know you're not supposed to think of those things until God sends you your true love and you enter a courtship, but lots of girls have an inkling ahead of time, especially if he's someone from your church."

"Right ... " I said.

"So, do you?"

I stared up at the dark ceiling, totally confused about how to handle this situation.

"Um...I don't think so. Or at least they haven't mentioned anyone. I guess they might want me to find someone on my own."

She propped herself up on her elbow and looked over at me. The glow from the barn light caught her eyes and they glittered.

"Really? But isn't that kind of risky?"

"Risky?" I repeated.

"Well, how could you be sure that you're marrying a good man? And how can you guard your heart while you're looking for him? If they just send you off into the world to find your own way, how will you be protected? What if you fall in love with the wrong person?"

Those were actually all perfectly valid questions. Beyond giving me a place to live and food to eat and money to buy stuff and the occasional lecture, at this point my parents basically did jack shit to make sure I was protected or that I didn't fall in love with the wrong person. Of course, that meant they also gave me the freedom to more or less do whatever I wanted.

It was kind of a trade-off.

"I don't know. They're hoping that I can deal with it all by myself, I guess," I said.

"Oh," said Abigail, lying back down on her side, hands folded to the side of her cheek. "That must be scary."

I thought about Blake and his face as he shoved me away from his car. "Yeah, I guess it is."

We were both silent for a moment.

"Faith?" she said, just as I began to assume she'd fallen asleep.

"Hmm?"

"What did you think of Beau? I mean, honestly. Don't fib."

I silently twisted the blanket in my hands.

"He … seems nice. It's nice that he's, you know, already kind of part of your family," I said, stretching for good things to say. Because what else could I tell her? If I admitted how gross and suspicious I found him, it would just make her feel bad. And I knew how much she wanted a happily ever after.

"You think so?"

"Sure," I replied. "But really, the important thing is what you think of him and how he makes you feel."

She was silent.

"Abigail?"

"He's a fine man," she said firmly.

"Yeah, you've said that already. What else?"

She sighed softly.

"You can't tell anyone about this or I'll … I'll completely disown you," she said with a small, sad laugh.

"Okay?" I prompted.

She turned over in bed so she was staring straight up at the ceiling.

"He's … well, he's said some things to me," she said. "In the past."

"Things?" I was confused. "Like what?"

"A few weeks ago, after he came over to talk to Daddy one afternoon, he … he came out to the barn while I was getting the chicken feed. No one else was around. And he came up behind me and put his hands on me … " Abigail's voice was beginning to quaver.

I caught my breath.

"He … he put his hands on you? Where?"

"Right here." In the darkness, I could just make out that she put her hands on her rib cage, below her breasts. "And he pulled me back and squeezed me so hard I almost couldn't breathe and then he whispered in my ear that … that … "

She stopped and took a deep breath. I waited in silent shock.

"He told me that I was defrauding, just by walking around in front of him, and that all he wanted was to put the sinful thoughts out of his head and be with me as a husband is with his wife. And then he kissed my cheek and … and squeezed me again … and told me it would be a bad idea to tell Daddy what had just happened, because Daddy would know it was my fault."

"Are you serious?" I asked. As if Abigail would joke about something like this.

She put her hands over her face. "Faith, it was so awful! I've felt so terrible about it ever since!"

"Was that the first time he ever did something like that?" I asked, barely recognizing my own dangerous voice.

She shook her head, hands still over her face. "No, there were a few other times."

"For how long?"

"For a while," she said. "Since Rachel and Elijah started courting, I guess, and he's been coming around. I try not to think about it. But...but that was the worst time."

Rage began to bloom in my chest. A rage like I hadn't felt since I came upon Blake and Caitlin Merriweather propped up against his car. My internal Faith-censor went straight out the window and flew ten miles across the cornfields and exploded in the sky.

"Abigail, this is unacceptable. That man is a complete molesting asshole and you should never talk to him again."

She took her hands off her face and looked at me. "Did you just say—"

I interrupted her. "No, really. The next time I see him I'm seriously going to kick him in the balls."

"Faith!" she said, with a shocked laugh.

"Did you tell your parents about this?"

"Nooo," she said slowly. "They really like him. They...they'll probably think it was my fault, just like he said."

"That's such BS!" I burst out. "How about Asher? Did you tell him?"

"No, of course not!" Abigail said quickly. "He'd...I don't know, he might try and fight Beau or something, and it would be bad for everyone. He can't do anything."

I propped myself up on my elbow, feeling ready to go into battle.

"Maybe someone *needs* to kick the crap out of him!"

"No, Asher would just get in trouble with Daddy. *Shhh*, please, it's not that big of a deal."

"Abigail! He *assaulted* you! Is that really something a good Christian man would do?"

She made a strangled sort of uncertain sound.

"No … I suppose not." She didn't sound convinced. "But *assault* is kind of exaggerating. And, I mean, I probably did do something to encourage him. Without knowing. Maybe my dress was too tight or I smiled too much—"

"No," I said. "It absolutely wasn't your fault! It was all him."

"I don't know … he's a good person in other ways, and—"

"You can't blame yourself for this," I insisted, my heart beating fast in my anger, my voice rising. "Beau is a gross old letch. Don't you see how he looks at you? Like you're a piece of meat? And all he did was brag about himself and act important. Just because he can recite some Bible passages and agrees with your dad about pre-tribulation Rapture or whatever doesn't make him a good guy. Or a good future husband. God, Abigail, how can you even consider marrying him after what he did to you?"

Abigail had gone still during my rant, her arms now crossed tightly against her chest.

"I think I've said too much," she whispered. "Thanks

for your support, Faith, but I've realized this is a private matter. I shouldn't have brought you into it."

I'd lost her. I'd pushed it too far and gotten out of character and I'd lost her.

"Abigail, I'm sorry, I just—"

"*I'm* sorry your parents don't consider it their duty to find you a husband. You know, I was under the impression that our families had similar beliefs about things like that." Her voice was icy. "The Lord punishes envy, you know."

"Are you trying to say I'm jealous of you? Because of Beau?" For a second, I couldn't help but marvel at the bizarre backward parallels in my weird life. I wished that I could call up Kelsey and Amanda right that minute and tell them about it.

"I've been wondering, for a while in fact, if we really are so much alike," Abigail said coolly.

I didn't really have anything to reply. She'd told me her secret, and all I ended up doing was screwing things up and driving her away. And now she was suspicious.

"Good night, Faith," she said, with finality, and turned to face the wall.

I stayed awake, my mind racing, long after her breathing turned deep and regular.

SEVENTEEN

When the alarm went off the next morning, I sat straight up in bed and turned to Abigail. It felt like I'd been completely conscious the entire night, going over my options, and I knew exactly what I was going to say.

"Abigail," I said, "I'm really sorry about what I said last night."

She rubbed her eyes and then looked at me, blond wisps framing her sleepy face. She didn't say anything.

"Remember what you told me, about asking for forgiveness?" I asked. "When I make a mistake, I mean. I'm really sorry and I hope you'll forgive me. The truth is, I *was* jealous. I wish I knew a guy like Beau who wanted to marry me. I wish my parents would find me a good man. And I was tired and cranky and I spoke out of envy. I'm sorry."

Even as the words came out of my mouth, I felt gross and disgusting. I was taking the chicken's way out. I was doing whatever I could to cover my ass and continue in my Faith lie, instead of being honest.

As I searched her face, Abigail gave me a small smile. And I felt like the worst person in the whole world. But I hoped that maybe this way, I could continue being her friend and maybe find a way to help her.

She got out of bed, came over, and grabbed my hands. "Of course I forgive you, Faith. It was very sweet of you to apologize like that. It's water under the bridge. Okay?"

I smiled back up at her, both relieved and hating myself. "Okay. Thank you."

"Don't mention it," she said.

I nodded.

"No seriously," she said, looking me right in the eye, an intensity in her face that I hadn't seen before. "Promise that you won't mention it. To anyone. Ever."

"I . . . promise," I said.

. . .

It was the hottest day of the summer so far. By eleven a.m., it was over ninety degrees, and my ridiculous long denim skirt stuck to the back of my thighs whenever I sat down. Sweat dripped off everyone's faces, even with all the fans in the house turned up to high. I longed for a pair of shorts and a tank top.

Mrs. Dean left to go to a doctor's appointment in the morning, so Abigail and I were in charge of the house. We fixed everyone sandwiches for lunch, and then I watched

Abigail and tried not to cringe as she gave a science lesson out of a book to the little kids. She was teaching them how dinosaurs had existed in the Garden of Eden, and how they had been wiped out in Noah's flood, their bones scattered across the world.

I didn't know whether to laugh or cry.

"But what did the dinosaurs eat in Eden?" asked Luke, who was seven.

"Coconuts!" said Abigail brightly. "Before the Fall of Man, dinosaurs were vegetarian! Isn't that amazing? God provided for all His creatures."

Before she could continue, Asher came through the front door with a giant, boyish smile on his face.

"I've rigged up a surprise for everyone," he told us, beaming. "Come and see."

Outside was a long blue tarp, positioned so that it was facing down a small hill in the front yard. At the top was a hose going full blast and, as we watched, Asher dumped some liquid soap into the streaming water. Instantly, the tarp was covered in slippery bubbles.

The smaller kids squealed in delight, jumping up and down. Chastity, holding Mercy, did a little dance and giggled.

"Come on, kids, let's go change!" Abigail said.

We tumbled upstairs, chattering happily. The boys dressed themselves in swim shorts and T-shirts, while all of us girls put on old tops and work skirts with shorts underneath. There were certainly no bikinis in this family.

But everyone lost all sense of decorum on the rigged-up slip-and-slide. The kids threw themselves down it on their bellies, screaming happily. Abigail and I slid down it together holding hands, the soap seeping into our hair and clothes. The water felt wonderful and cool on my skin, and I finally stopped sweating.

I heard Abigail screech, and I looked over to see Asher with the hose pointed at her, laughing.

"Hey, no fair!" I said. He turned to look at me, grinning, and then sprayed me directly in the face.

"Asher, stop that!" said Abigail. She ran to grab the hose out of his hands and then threw it to me. "Get him, Faith!"

So I sprayed Asher back as he fought against Abigail, all of us giggling. He got away from his sister, yanked the hose away from me, and chased us both around with the hose, slipping on the wet grass and laughing.

"Truce! Truce!" Abigail called after a few minutes, and we all stopped in place, panting.

Then Luke called to Abigail to slide with him, so she smiled at us and walked away. "Don't let him get you, Faith," she said over her shoulder.

My hair was plastered to my head and neck as I bent over, hands on my knees, hardly able to breathe after running around and dodging the hose. My shirt was stuck to my body and I tried to pull it loose so it wasn't quite so formfitting. I smiled up at Asher, seeing that he was watching me.

He smiled back, and it hit me once again just how unselfconsciously gorgeous he was. Especially when he was happy, with dimples in his cheeks and crinkles around his mouth, his blue eyes dancing in the sun. His shirt was also soaked and dripping, accentuating every muscle of his chest and arms. And his tanned skin glowed like he was lit from within.

I couldn't help it anymore. It was time to admit I was crushing on him. And hard.

"Having fun?" he asked in a husky voice. Some part of my brain registered that there were noisy kids running all around us, but it suddenly felt like we were the only two people on the planet.

I nodded. "Lots of fun. We don't do anything like this at home."

He took a step closer. "Good. I'm glad you're having a nice time here."

I took a deep, gulping breath. Then I reached over and plucked a stray blade of grass off his shoulder. He jumped a little at my touch.

"You're a good brother to set all this up," I said. "The kids really adore you."

He shrugged a bit. "I try. Everyone needs to let loose and play a little, I think."

"You're right."

He was staring at me. "F-Faith, you ... " he said slowly. "What?"

"You have some, um, dirt on your cheek," he said. And then he licked his thumb and reached over, gently grazing my face.

I couldn't look away from his eyes. They held me in place.

"Thanks," I said softly, realizing that I was leaning

toward him like a tree in a strong wind. He was leaning toward me, too.

Then it broke.

"Daddy's home!" screamed some of the kids.

Behind me, I heard the sound of a truck door slam. Asher and I both blinked, the moment lost. He looked suddenly terrified and backed quickly away from me.

"What's all this about?" said Mr. Dean in his jovial way, though I detected an edge to his voice. He was staring hard at me, and then looked at Asher, who was busy turning off the hose at a spigot on the house. "Asher and Abigail, please tell me what's going on here."

All the little kids were gathered around their father, dripping on his work boots.

"Asher set up a slide!" announced Luke.

"I see that, son," said Mr. Dean. "But the question is, why?"

"Because it's fun!" said Martha, wiping soaked blond wisps from her face.

"But did you all get your work done before you played?" asked Mr. Dean sternly, crossing his arms. "Were you faithful and productive first, before you turned to having fun?"

The children were all suddenly guilty-looking. Abigail, with little Mercy perched on her hip and a free hand on Martha's head, looked particularly distraught.

"Oh, Daddy, we were just playing in the water because it's so hot in the house," she began to explain, but he held up his index finger to silence her.

"You did not have permission to do this. Asher, get over here right now."

Asher seemed to brace himself as he walked over to join his siblings. All nine of them looked cowed and deflated, in a small herd around their father.

I hovered over by the porch, unsure of what to do or where to look, my clothes soapy and uncomfortable.

Mr. Dean was talking in a low voice to his children. I couldn't make out exactly what he was saying, but his tone was harsh and angry. The words "obedience" and "duty" drifted over to me.

He sent all the younger kids into the house to rinse off and change, and then laid into Asher and Abigail for another five minutes. By the end, Abigail was crying, and Asher had his arms crossed so tightly against his chest that it looked painful, his fingers digging into his own skin.

Abigail was allowed to leave, and she came up to me with a tremulous look on her face. "Sorry you had to witness that, Faith. We shouldn't have set up the slide without asking Daddy, of course. Let's go change."

As we walked up the porch stairs, I turned to see Mr. Dean with one hand on Asher's shoulder and the other pointing angrily in my direction.

"Temptation" was the only word I heard.

Mr. Dean had seen Asher touch me. And I knew that was seriously bad news.

EIGHTEEN

Dinner was silent and awkward. Mr. Dean wouldn't look anyone in the eye, just sternly said grace and ate his food without talking. Mrs. Dean had returned from her doctor's appointment looking tired and run-down, and no one filled her in on what had happened.

As soon as I could get away from the dishes, I escaped outside for some time alone. The tension was too much for me to handle.

At home, when there was drama, we could all just go hole up in separate parts of the house. But there was no place to retreat in a family of this size. No place for privacy or quiet.

I was standing on the far side of the barn, watching the quickly appearing stars over the back field, when Asher turned the corner and ran right into me.

"Shit, sorry!" I said without thinking, at the same time that he said, "Oh, excuse me!"

We both stood still, staring at each other.

"Wait ... " he said, trailing off, and then swallowed. "What did you just say?"

I bit my lip, distracted from my foul-language screw-up by the way his eyes gleamed in the fading daylight. All I could think about was how it had felt earlier in the day when his warm thumb grazed my face.

"Um, shoot?" I suggested after a moment. "I think I just said shoot."

He kept gazing at me, his expression unreadable. And then slowly, surely, he started to smile. It was a mischievous, boyish sort of smile, and his tense face was transformed.

"You did *not* just say shoot, Faith," he said.

I couldn't help but grin back at him, even though the feeling of a magnetic pull toward his body unsettled me.

"Whatever, I totally did!"

"Did not. You cussed!"

"You can't prove anything. No one else was here!" Without thinking, I reached over and gave him a playful poke in the chest, like I would have if I were attempting to flirt with a boy back home.

Well, back when I used to attempt flirting. Since Blake, I hadn't felt comfortable enough around guys to even make much eye contact. Let alone touch anyone. But there was certainly something different about *this* particular boy.

As soon as I touched him, Asher turned away and

leaned back against the barn. It was as if an invisible brick wall came down between us.

Oops.

"Sorry," I said, glad for the dim, pinkish light so he couldn't see the red of my face. "I didn't mean to..."

"N-n-no, it's okay," Asher said, tripping over his words and still not looking at me. "I mean, after all, earlier I... but you know, we really sh-shouldn't—"

"We shouldn't be out here alone," I finished for him. "You're right."

Neither of us made a move to leave.

"Because if someone from my family came back here and saw us together, it w-wouldn't..."

"It wouldn't look good," I said. "You're totally right about that."

Still, neither of us moved.

I leaned back against the barn near him, not quite letting my arm touch his, and we looked at the stars together. It was a quiet moment, with no sound except the crickets in the fields, the sleepy clucking of a few chickens, and a dog barking somewhere far away. And, of course, my wild heart thumping in my ears like an accompanying bass line.

"Because the thing is, Faith," Asher said in a sudden rush. "The thing is, you're a really nice, sweet girl. And... I'm not."

I chuckled. "Well, it's true you're certainly not a girl, at least!"

He turned to look at me, his eyes wide again, and laughed. I'm sure he wasn't used to talking to girls in this playful way. Except for maybe the girls he'd met in his college classes. I hoped he liked smart-ass girls like me.

"We just really shouldn't be out here alone," he continued, and sighed morosely. "This is just what Dad yelled at me about. I really don't want him to be right all the time, but he always is."

"Right about what?" I asked.

Asher shrugged and looked at the sky again. "He believes it's my duty as a Christian man to help keep good Christian girls on as holy of a path as possible, because otherwise they could become impure. And impure women are temptresses. And if I allow one into my heart, I could be defrauded."

I turned my head and rolled my eyes to the dark. Yes, *obviously* it was the man's job to keep us weak-willed women in our place, otherwise we might cause men's downfall, just like good old Eve. Even in that moment, I couldn't help but be disgusted by the stupid dichotomy— that there were some people who really believed women could only be sluts or saints. Delicate objects who couldn't think for themselves, or evil whores out to ruin men. We couldn't just be human.

And, well, I guess I already knew which category these people would put me in. If they knew who I really was, that is.

I looked back at Asher and, without thinking any further about it, decided to take a risk.

"Is that what *you* believe, though?"

He looked at me, his brow knitted together. "Well, we're supposed to, right? Isn't that following a Christian path?"

"I guess," I replied. "I've been thinking lately, though. I can't speak for every girl in the world, of course, but I believe we were given free will and I've decided that I feel pretty responsible for my own path."

My own path that had led directly to naked webcam pictures and school suspensions and social pariah-hood, that is. Still, at least it was a path that was all *mine*.

"I mean, I appreciate your concern and all, but I feel like my ..." I searched for the words from my bank of fundamentalist-speak. "I feel like *I* should be the primary one who should purpose to protect the sanctity of my purity. Not, you know ... *you*. I mean, you protect your own purity or whatever, but mine is my own business."

Asher gave me a grim smile, searching my eyes, and then looked down at his shoes and scuffed them in the dirt a few times. "But oh, Faith, if you only knew."

"Knew what?"

"My doubts," he said.

"Doubts?"

He paused, chewed on his lip for a moment, and then looked back at me darkly.

"All these thoughts I can't seem to stop myself from thinking. And how weak I am. You'd be much more concerned for your purity, if you knew. You wouldn't be standing out here with me where no one can see us."

My heart began to pick up again, and my palms started to sweat a bit. It felt like all my common sense and self-preservation had fled the scene with that one dark, wanting look he'd given me.

"Why wouldn't I want to be here with you?" I asked, allowing some flirt to creep into my voice.

"Because," he said softly. "Because all I want to do ... "

I stepped closer to him, staring up at his face, every nerve ending in my body irrationally aching to touch him and pull him close.

"What do you want to do?" I asked softly.

He lifted one of his hands. It was trembling a little. I looked down at his hand, then back at his face, which was tense and distraught like he was in physical pain. I lifted my own hand and put it softly against his, allowing my fingers to slide between his fingers as I watched his eyes.

"Asher?" I said. I could feel heat pouring from his body. "What do you want to do?"

And without warning he leaned toward me, gathered my body in his arms, and began to kiss my lips and face. Great gasping kisses, like he was dying and I could save him.

"*Faith ... Faith ... Faith,*" he murmured into my mouth, holding me tighter, spinning me around and pushing me back against the side of the barn.

At first, all I wanted to do was kiss Asher back wildly, press my body against his and dig my fingers into his soft hair. But I was so shocked that he'd actually followed through that I didn't move. I just stood in place and let it happen.

He kissed his way down my cheek and buried his face in my neck and I couldn't help but moan a little, getting lost in the moment. Even though I knew what we were doing was against his beliefs, even though I knew he'd regret it later and I would feel bad and shameful.

His lips were so warm and insistent in the curve between my shoulder and throat. I pulled his face up from my neck and pressed my mouth to his, matching him kiss for kiss until we both became breathless. One of his hands went up to cup the back of my head, protecting me from the hard side of the barn. His other hand was on the small of my back, then moving lower and lower and pulling my body more firmly toward his...

Without warning, my brain yanked me violently back to the last time I'd been this close to someone. Blake. Who had turned my affection and desire around and tried to destroy me. Who had treated my body like something to be used. My stomach turned over sickeningly and my head went dizzy. I stopped kissing Asher back and put my hands against his chest to push him away.

"Asher—" was all I said, and he stopped immediately. His body went rigid under my hands.

He pulled away from me, breathing hard, his eyes wide. We stared at each other for a moment, and then he started pacing back and forth in front of me, running his hands through his hair.

"What did I do?" he whispered. "How could I have done that to you?"

"What? No, Asher, it's okay!" I tried to catch one of his wrists in my hand. He shook me off. "No, really, it's okay!" I insisted.

"How could I have done that to you?" he repeated, panicked. "What kind of an awful man am I?"

"Seriously, it's really fine!" I said. I was only lying a little. I wanted to tell him so badly about who I was and what I'd been through. About how I was also completely confused about what was going on between us. And that I wanted to figure it all out together. I desperately wanted to simply *talk*, but there was so much in the way of being honest.

"It's not fine!" he yelled back, his voice breaking. "I'm a sinner. I'm worthless! I just defrauded an innocent girl like . . . like some sort of . . . of fornicator! Dad would tell me I'm going to hell for this! He'd be right!"

"*Shhh,* please!" I felt guilty tears come into my eyes. "You're not going to hell for kissing!"

He whirled back around and came toward me, and then he was kneeling at my feet like a supplicant, holding onto my hand.

"Will you forgive me, Faith? P-Please say you'll forgive me or I don't know how I'll live with myself."

"Asher, you're really freaking out way too much about this! It's not like I didn't have anything to do with it . . . I encouraged you! I kissed you back! Plus, you don't even know—"

"I can't believe it happened again," he said, cutting me off. He wasn't even listening to me. He was too caught up in his own trauma, and my words were making no impact.

I sighed.

"Okay! Listen! Okay, Asher, I forgive you!" I said to

the top of his head. "Please, would you ... please just let go of me."

He reluctantly released my hand and I turned to hurry back to the house, trying not to cry.

"I'm so sorry, Faith!" he called softly after me.

NINETEEN

Everyone was beginning to gather noisily in the living room for evening prayers when I got back into the house.

The prospect of listening to Mr. Dean drone on and on from the Bible made me feel ill, and I knew I had to make an excuse and get out of it.

I found Abigail, who was just taking off her apron to hang in the pantry. She gave me a small smile that didn't meet her eyes, and I knew that she was still embarrassed about how her dad had yelled at all of them earlier. But making out with Asher had neatly divided everything in my life into a before and after, and the slide in the front yard seemed so far away.

"I'm sorry, Abigail. I'm not feeling well," I told her. "Do you think it would be okay if I go lie down?"

"You do look flushed," she said, ever the caretaker, her

sad look turning worried. "Do you want anything? Water? Some ginger ale?"

"No, I don't—" I stopped when the back door opened. It was Asher, looking tired and hunched over. He glanced at me once, his eyes distraught, and then walked toward the living room. I watched him go, wishing I could run over and tackle him and hold him down until I could convince him he wasn't broken.

Abigail also watched him walk away, and then turned to look at me with an indecipherable expression on her face. "You're sure you don't want anything?"

"Yes," I said. "I think maybe I just need to rest."

"Of course," she said, and put a hand on my arm. "I'll tell the others and we'll say a prayer for you. I hope you feel better ... we're having company again tomorrow."

I looked at her. "Who?"

She pursed her lips for a moment and sighed. "Beau. I guess he's ... he's coming to speak to my father before dinner."

I gasped involuntarily, putting a hand over my mouth. "What does that—" I said through my fingers.

"I don't know what it means," she interrupted. "But I'm sure it will be lovely to see him again. The little kids really do like him."

I searched her face, looking for any trace of disingenuousness, but she seemed to mean it. Or she was covering up her discomfort so well that it was impossible to detect.

"Right," I said. "Lovely."

I tried not to run up the stairs too quickly, and once I

got into Abigail's room, I literally collapsed face-first onto the homemade quilt.

I was completely exhausted and lost. The confusion had built up to almost unbearable levels.

It had become obvious that I had to make a decision. As I saw it, there were two choices. I could go on letting Abigail think her eventual engagement to Beau was a good idea. I could allow Asher to think that he had done a horrible thing and tarnished me forever. I could continue being a passive observer in the drama, playing the part of pure Faith while everyone crashed and burned around me.

Or I could tell the truth. And I could try to stand and fight for Abigail, and do for her what I hadn't allowed anyone to do for me.

. . .

I dozed off as I was thinking things over and only woke up when Abigail turned the light off when she went to bed. I lay in the dark, listening to her breathe, until I was sure she had been fallen into a deep sleep. And then I quietly got up and wrapped myself in a robe.

The house was silent as I crept down the stairs. Only the ticking of a grandfather clock and the hum of the fridge in the kitchen were audible.

Asher's room was in the basement. I'd seen the door when Abigail sent me downstairs to get something from storage. He was the only member of the family with his own room. Abigail told me it was because Mr. Dean thought he would be a bad influence on the younger boys, and it was a sort of punishment to be so far away from everyone else.

I didn't see how getting your own room was a punishment, but Abigail seemed to feel sorry for him.

There was a dim sliver of light underneath his door, but no sounds from within.

I hesitated for a long moment, my knuckles poised to knock on the door. I almost turned around and tiptoed back upstairs. But then I thought of Abigail and how she'd cried as she described what Beau had done to her. And for a moment, I thought of Blake.

And I knocked.

After a few seconds, Asher opened the door and looked out at me. His eyes went wide.

"Faith! What do you think you're doing?" he whispered.

"I have to talk to you," I said.

He ran his hands through his hair, which was sticking up everywhere in that disturbingly attractive way. I tried to catch a glimpse of his room behind him, but he was blocking my view.

"You shouldn't be down here! Did anyone see you? This is such a bad idea, especially after—"

"Listen, this isn't really about what happened earlier."

He paused for a moment.

"It's not?"

"No. Well, we probably should talk about that at some point. But not now. This is about Abigail."

"Abigail? What about her? Is she sick?"

"She's okay right now. But can I please just come in so we can talk for a minute?"

He glanced all around him as if the floor or walls would provide an answer for what he was supposed to do. Then he looked at me, almost fearfully, like I was some sort of succubus.

"Look," I said, tired of the whole purity business now that I had a mission. "I'm not going to let you corrupt me more or whatever, okay? You're safe."

For now, anyway.

His scared look broke, and he almost smiled. "Oh, I'm safe? You're sure?"

"Positive."

"Well, come in, I guess," he said, opening the door a little wider. "But just for a minute."

His room was painfully small and neat, like a monk's cell. Just a twin bed and a desk and a dresser, in an unpainted drywalled space that was probably a large repurposed closet. There was a little window up near the ceiling that let in a shaft of pale moonlight. He had no posters or pictures on the bare gray walls, and no books except a Bible, sitting open on the middle of his desk. It was worn and the edges of the pages were frayed, as if it had been leafed through many times.

"What are you reading?" I asked, going over to look at the pages.

"Matthew," he replied.

"Which part?" I asked, as if I would know.

Asher shut his eyes and recited from memory.

"'But I say unto you, that whosoever looketh on a woman to lust after her hath committed adultery with her already in his heart.'" He opened his eyes and looked at me sadly. "My father told me it was…it was applicable to my situation. I'm memorizing a big part of it."

"Oh," I said, stepping away from his desk like the book might bite me. "Right, that verse."

"And, in terms of that verse, you being here is not particularly helpful," Asher said. "Alone. In my room. In the middle of the night. What was it you wanted to talk about?"

I sat in his desk chair and looked at him, trying to figure out how to break it to him. But there was no way to go about this except straight through.

"Asher, Beau did something to Abigail."

"Something? What do you mean, something?"

"He's cornered her alone a couple of times," I said, and took a deep breath. "And…and put his hands on her."

Asher looked at me blankly for a minute, and I watched as a wave of comprehension crossed his face. He sat down heavily on his bed.

"Without her permission," I added, just in case that needed to be clarified.

Asher nodded dully, his eyes looking at something far away. "Of course. Abigail's a nice girl. She would never…"

He trailed off, and we were both silent for a moment. I waited for him to get angry, to stand up and storm around the little room and swear revenge. But he just sat there, staring at nothing, looking more like a lost boy than a nineteen-year-old almost-man.

"I told her I wouldn't tell anyone," I finally said, to get the conversation going again. "But what Beau did is awful and wrong and I feel like someone in the family should know. I mean, it sounds like he's probably going to ask to marry her, and he's obviously a total ass—I mean, terrible person. You have to tell your dad, Asher. You can't let it happen."

Asher stayed quiet.

"Asher? You can't let it happen!" I repeated.

"Right…" he said slowly.

"So what are you going to do?" I asked, getting frustrated. "Are you going to tell your dad? Will you go beat Beau up? I'll totally come with you."

He blinked and looked at me, as if finally realizing I was there.

"I don't know what I'm going to do," he said, and stood up. "A-A-And you should go back upstairs."

"Don't you want to, I don't know, talk it over or something?" I asked. "Don't you have any questions or—"

"No," he said, shortly. "I have to think."

"Think?" I couldn't believe what I was hearing. Here I thought Asher was some honorable guy, so concerned with doing the right thing, and he was acting like his sister being assaulted was just something he had to quietly mull over for a while.

He nodded and I stood up. "Fine then," I said, with some hostility. "You think for a while."

Chicken, I wanted to add.

"Faith, please," he said. "I have to figure it out. This

isn't something you run off to deal with without thinking it through and praying on it."

I put my hands on my hips. "Look, Asher. Abigail is my friend. I'm only here for a little while longer and the thought of her ending up with that creep makes me feel physically ill. I want to help her, but I don't know how. I need you to do something."

"She may be your friend, but she's *my* sister," he replied, looking at me pleadingly. "And this is *my* family. I appreciate your concern and the fact you told me about what happened, but at this point, it's not really your business. Or your place to help."

Ugh, not that men-in-charge crap. Not now. I couldn't stomach it anymore.

"It's not my place *as a girl* to worry about what happens to her? Is that what you're trying to say?" I said. "Because the men in your family are doing such a bang-up job of protecting her. Obviously."

His mouth fell open in disbelief.

I walked up to him and stood right in his face. "Do something about it, Asher. Help her. Please. She needs you. Can't you see that?"

Asher looked down into my eyes, which I knew were flashing and tearful. He stared, and I stared back. Neither of us blinked. He leaned forward just slightly.

And suddenly I was kissing him. Again.

TWENTY

I went through the next day in a daze. My brain felt over-loaded with information and complications, and all I wanted to do was find someplace quiet and lonely to sit and think.

But there was Abigail, trying to act like her normal cheerful self. There was a desperate shininess to her eyes, though, and I could tell that underneath she was in a panic, thinking about the reason behind Beau's visit tonight.

"Are you okay?" I asked her, about a hundred times.

"Of course!" she'd reply, far too brightly. "Why wouldn't I be?"

And then there was Asher, throwing secret smiles at me, making my heart flutter and my stomach drop at the same time, creating such a weird combination of complete infatuation and total guilt and weird annoyance whenever

I was around him. I felt drained of energy whenever he got within ten feet of me.

The night before, we'd stood in his room and kissed for ten whole glorious minutes, until I got control of myself and rushed out the door before he could say anything. Abigail was softly snoring upstairs, and I slipped into bed feeling both exhilarated and like an idiot.

How could I be doing this? How could I trust a guy who didn't even know who I really was? Especially when I knew he believed that what we were doing was sinful. Was he just getting off on how forbidden it was, or did he actually care about me?

I wanted to ignore his existence while other people were around, but the fact that all I wanted to do was yank him close and make out for at least three days straight created somewhat of a problem.

And the way he would glance at me, full of longing, convinced me he was having a similar issue.

That afternoon, we found a few minutes to speak alone when we were out in the garden picking some early cherry tomatoes. Abigail had gone into the house to find more baskets, and I stepped nearer to where Asher was crouching.

"So have you figured it out?" I whispered.

"Figured out what?" he replied, not looking at me, but putting his warm hand on my bare foot. "How we end up kissing all the time?"

I laughed softly and crouched down next to him.

"That's not exactly what I meant, but while we're on the subject, how *does* that keep happening?"

He sighed, standing up straight to wipe his face with the bandana again. It was such a cute gesture that it took all the willpower I had not to reach out and hug his legs.

"I don't know," he said, looking down at me. "I … can't seem to resist you."

"That feeling is mutual," I said.

His brow furrowed. "It's wrong, you know," he said. "You can't keep letting me do that to you. It's dishonorable."

"So now it's my fault?" I asked.

"Your … your heart should be wh-whole," he said, struggling for the words. "For your husband."

Ugh. Time to change the subject. "What I was really wondering is if you've figured out what you're going to do about Beau."

He moved away, and didn't reply for so long that I finally picked up a half-rotten tomato that had fallen on the ground and chucked it at his arm.

"Hey!" he said, throwing it back at me.

"I'm serious," I said. "What are you going to do?"

"I guess I need to talk to Abigail about it," he said. "I don't know when."

"But Beau's coming here tonight and—"

"Faith, I know that. But we don't know why or what's going on. It … it could just be a normal dinner and we're getting all worked up for—"

"It's not, you know it's not! Abigail said he's never come on his own like this, without Rachel and Elijah. And he's never come this early. Your dad is making a big deal about some conversation they're going to have."

Asher sighed. "I know."

I stood up, no longer caring if anyone was observing us.

"I meant what I said before. If you don't do anything about this, I will!"

"Shhh, Faith!" he said, looking around anxiously. "I believe you, okay? But I just really think I need to talk to Abigail first—"

"But then she'll know that I told you!"

"Maybe I could get it out of her some other way." He glanced anxiously around the garden, and I felt terrible. I was beginning to think I shouldn't have told him anything.

"Maybe," I said, and sighed. I looked over at the house and saw that Mr. Dean was watching us from the kitchen window. His face was unreadable. When he noticed me looking at him, he turned away.

"Asher, what would you do if you told your dad and he pushed ahead with it anyway?" I asked. "What if he still made Abigail marry that guy? What if he found someone for you to marry who *you* didn't like?"

Please say you'd fight it. Please say you'd laugh in his face and leave this craziness behind.

I knew it was an irrational and cruel thought. This life was what Asher knew and believed in. Why would he leave?

He glanced over at me, and then off across the garden toward the fields. "I don't know. That's why I'm having such a hard time figuring this out. Because I guess I'd do what I'm supposed to do. Stay with my family and be a good son."

My heart sank.

"Even if…"

"If what?"

"If you figured out you disagreed with your dad? And if you really wanted a…a different life?"

"Like what kind of life?"

A normal life.

"I don't know…like in a city or something."

"What do you know about living in a city?"

I shrugged. "It's just something I've thought about. I mean, I'm sure not everyone who lives in cities is bad. I bet there are all kinds of people. Good people, even. People you would like."

He watched me with that same quizzical look, like he was trying to categorize me and was failing at it.

"I guess I've thought about it sometimes," he admitted. "But it would mean the end."

"The end?"

"The end of being his son."

"Maybe he'll surprise you?" I suggested, thinking of my parents, who hadn't disowned me for my stupid mistakes. And at least seemed to forget about them for periods of time.

"Doubt it," Asher said.

"Doubt what?" said Abigail from nearby. She had snuck up behind us.

Both of us turned to face her entirely too quickly, and she gave us a suspicious look.

"What's going on here?" she said.

Asher and I looked at each other, then back at her.

"Um…" I said.

"We were talking about Beau," said Asher. "We were talking about tonight."

"Oh." Abigail's eyes narrowed even more as she looked at me. "What about Beau?"

I glanced at Asher, sure that we both radiated guilt. Abigail caught on instantly.

"Did you tell him, Faith?" she demanded. "Did you… I can't believe you did that when I asked you not to!"

"She's worried," said Asher with a helpless shrug. "We both are. I've just… I've just never liked him very much either, okay? I wasn't surprised. And I just want for you to—"

"Faith, I told you that stuff in confidence," Abigail hissed at me, with more hostility then I'd previously thought she had in her entire body. "I guess that was a mistake."

"I'm sorry. I couldn't stay quiet," I said desperately, looking from her to Asher. I felt so awkward, being in the middle of two siblings. Me and my big mouth had caused this.

No, Beau and his grossness caused this, said a voice inside me.

"I was thinking that I should… I should tell Dad," Asher was saying. "He should know about what Beau did."

"What?" Abigail crossed her arms tightly. "No. Just… absolutely not. Don't you dare say anything to Daddy."

"But, Abi—"

"I will never forgive you," she said, cutting him off. "And how do you know you're not getting in the way of God's plan for me? How would you feel about that?"

Asher tried to put his hand on her shoulder. "But how do you know, Abi—"

"It was my fault, okay?" She shook his hand off angrily. "Whatever happened was my fault and I don't want Daddy to know. If you tell him, I'll … I'll tell him about you two."

Asher and I stared at her.

I didn't like the way she said that. My stomach clenched.

"Because look at you," she spat, shaking her head slowly. "You're practically … canoodling out here! And don't think I didn't notice you two last night, coming in from the barn."

"Abigail, you have the wrong idea … " I said, even though she really didn't have the wrong idea at all.

"This is just great!" Abigail snapped, glaring at her brother. "How dare you try and get into my business and tell me what to do when you're so weak and worldly. You're supposed to be a leader for me and someone to look up to, but all I see is weakness."

Asher looked stung to the core, his eyes wide. After blinking at her for a few moments, he turned and walked quickly away, heading for the barn.

"You know it's true, Asher," Abigail called after him. "While I'm praying and striving to continue on a godly path to marriage, you aren't even *trying*."

We both watched him go.

"Did you hear me?" she yelled. "If you say anything to anyone, I'll … I'll tell! About you!"

Asher didn't turn around. He disappeared into the open barn door, his shoulders slumped.

"Please, Abigail, you need to—"

She turned toward me and held up her hand. "No. Do not dare," she said through clenched teeth, her face red. "Do not even presume to think you can tell me what to do or act like you know the first thing about what I need to do."

And then she looked me square in the eye and said one word. Like it was the worst word in the whole English language.

"*Dylan.*"

TWENTY-ONE

I blinked at her, feeling weak in the legs.

"What?" I said, hoping I just had an auditory hallucination.

"I know the truth," Abigail said. "Your name isn't Faith. You're not from southern Wisconsin. I bet you're probably not even a Christian. You're just some weird girl who thought it would be funny to come here and gawk and pretend to be someone else for a while."

It's very possible that my heart stopped for a moment.

"Abigail, please don't—"

"SHUT UP!" she screamed, closing her eyes tight.

I glanced over at the porch, where several of the little kids had assembled and were watching us with interest. At least Asher had run away. I couldn't imagine facing both of them at once.

"How long have you known?" I finally asked, my voice cracking.

"Since this morning," she said. "I was in my room. Your mom called your cell phone and I picked it up, planning to take it to you. But then she asked for Dylan and I said 'Dylan who?' and she said 'Dylan Mahoney, the owner of this phone.' Apparently she thinks you're at some sort of camp in Springfield, which was interesting. I didn't correct her, so she probably doesn't suspect anything. She asked that you call her back."

Well, this is just great. Thanks a lot, Mom.

"And while you and Asher were out here having your little powwow about my life, I decided to Google the name Dylan Mahoney."

I stared down at the ground, feeling like I'd just had the air sucked out of my lungs by a vacuum cleaner. It was obvious what that meant, and what she had found. "Oh."

"*Oh* is right," she said. "You know, what you told me before makes so much more sense now. I understand why your friends don't want anything to do with you. I understand why you cuss and don't seem to really know the Word. There are naked pictures of you all over the Internet! It's the most awful thing I've ever seen. I had to immediately erase my browser history so Mama wouldn't see what I looked at!"

I glanced at her face, still so pretty and wholesome even in her justified rage. It was all over. I was right back where I had began. Alone.

I sighed in resignation. "You're right. I sent those pictures to my boyfriend at the time, and when we broke up, he sent them out to everyone and it was awful. And shameful. I was an idiot. So, go ahead and say it then."

She squinted at me, looking taken aback.

"Say ... what?"

"Go ahead and call me a whore. A harlot. A ... a Jezebel or whatever you would call someone like me. I know that's what you want to say. And it's not like it wouldn't be true. It's not like I haven't heard it before."

Abigail crossed her arms and shook her head, eyes looking toward the sky. "That's what you'd expect me to do, isn't it?"

I shrugged. "Isn't that the truth, though? And isn't lying a sin?"

And without a word, Abigail sat down. Right in the middle of the garden path, next to the tomatoes. She hugged her knees to her chest and stared straight ahead toward the back field, looking deflated.

Surprised, I sat down in the next row over, watching her through the leaves of the plants. The sun was shining down on us and the warm breeze ruffled our hair. I dug my bare feet into the soft soil, feeling it slide between my toes. Except for what we'd just said to each other, the moment was perfect.

"You know what the funny thing is?" Abigail said, sounding almost amused. "I wasn't planning on telling anyone about you."

"You weren't?" I was shocked.

She looked over at me with a sad ghost of a smile. "No. For two reasons. One, because I thought maybe I could still be a good influence on you and maybe even lead you to the Christ, or at least to some self-respect. Because *obviously* you need some sort of help there."

I almost chuckled, even in that horrible moment. The self-respect thing was true enough.

"And the second reason?" I asked.

"Faith... I mean, *Dylan*... even though I barely know who you really are and even though you're a liar and a sinner and you told my secrets..." She stopped and took a deep gulping breath. "You're actually the best friend I've ever had. And even after all this, I just... I really don't think you're a terrible person at all."

We regarded each other through the tomato plants. I found myself breathing through that pre-crying pain in my lungs, trying to will the tears not to come and humiliate me.

"Abigail, you're my best friend, too," I said. I felt a line of tears slip down my cheek and I wiped it away quickly, embarrassed. "And even though I've lied, and even though I don't know the first thing about the Bible and you don't know the psycho details of my stupid life, you do know... *me*. I know that sounds crazy, but it's true."

Abigail put her chin on her knees and looked at me.

"I believe you."

I was so surprised, I couldn't think of what to say for a moment.

"So, um, what happens now?" I eventually asked.

She shrugged. "I have no idea anymore. I don't know what to do. I've been praying and praying."

"And?"

Abigail shrugged and glanced at the sky again. "Nothing. The Lord seems to want me to figure this one out on my own."

"Do you … " I hesitated. "Do you think He wants you to forgive me?"

She gave a short laugh. "Um, probably. That's sort of what He's all about, if you get right down to it."

"I guess," I said. "I mean, you're the expert."

"'Forbearing one another, and forgiving one another, if any man have a quarrel against any: even as Christ forgave you, so also do ye,'" quoted Abigail.

We sat in silence again, and I realized that some giant chunk of tension had been released from the base of my spine. I hadn't even realized it had been there until it was gone. The worst had happened, but the sky hadn't come crashing down and I had survived.

So with nothing else left to lose, I decided to keep talking.

"Abigail, I'm really, really sorry about telling Asher your secret," I said. "But he's your brother and I'm just so worried about you."

"I know," she said with a sigh.

"So, what about Beau? What about what he did to you? And what he wants?"

Abigail pulled her knees in even tighter.

"It'd kind of weird, you know? If you weren't who you are, if you were really part of my world, there's no way I could actually tell you this. But … I just don't know. I should be happy … I *have* to be happy. This is what I want for my life. This is what my parents want. But Beau is just … not what I was picturing. Not at all. And I wonder if it's punishment, if the Lord is showing me that He is in control of my life, not me. That I need to submit to His will. But I just don't know, I don't … "

Tears were slipping down her cheeks now, leaving wet spots on her denim skirt. I reached through the leaves of the tomato plants and put my hand on her arm.

"For whatever it's worth, I'll still be your friend. Whatever you choose."

She nodded slowly, not speaking. I took my hand back.

"Can I ask one thing, though?" she said. "Just one."

"Yes, please. Anything," I said.

Our teary eyes met again, and she looked at me fiercely.

"Don't break my brother's heart. You've made a fool out of me, but don't do it to him. He's already so confused and has been hurt so badly."

I bit my lip and then said, "Believe me, hurting him is the last thing I want to do."

"Okay, well, then one more thing," she said. "You have to tell him who you really are."

I sighed and watched a ladybug crawl ponderously up my arm. "But won't that break his heart?"

"Not if he really adores you."

I looked over at her sharply. "Adores me?"

Abigail shrugged. "It shows in the way he looks at you. Anyone can see it."

"But—"

"Do you care for him?"

I thought of Asher's handsome face, his strong arms around me, the way it felt like he could look right into my eyes with no trace of deceit or guile because he didn't have an ounce of that in him. I thought of how I wasn't scared when I was kissing him, because I knew he was good, because he always wanted to do what he believed was the right thing, because I'd seen him with his family and knew how kind and gentle he was, even when he thought no one was watching.

And I thought of how bright his face could be when he was looking at me, like I made him feel happy as well.

Even though there were entire oceans of things between us, an eternity of things we'd still need to figure out about each other, I couldn't stand the idea of hurting him.

"Yes. Even though I've only known him for a week, I care about him a lot. But… don't you disapprove? Aren't you concerned about the fact that I'm not… like your family?"

"Look," she said, shaking her head. "I just want my brother to be happy. He's been miserable for months and, to be honest, I don't think this"—she gestured to indicate the farm—"is ever going to make him happy. And if you, Dylan-of-wherever-you're-from, are what he wants, then I'm not going to stand in his way. In fact, I think you could be good for each other. Maybe you could make each other better people."

"But your dad will stand in the way," I pointed out.

She laughed a little, morosely. "I think my father will stand in the way of whatever Asher wants to do if he doesn't exactly follow Daddy's vision. And Daddy's vision is almost impossible to live up to. That's just how Daddy is, for better or worse."

"But if you think that, why are you—"

She interrupted me. "Don't. It's not the same."

"But—" I said, frustrated.

"No. It's different for girls. Asher can head off into the world and do what he needs to do. But my place is here. The Bible itself says my place is here, in training to be a helpmeet to my husband." She took a deep breath and closed her eyes. "'Wives, submit to your husbands, as to the Lord. For the husband is the head of the wife even as Christ is the head of the church.'"

I cringed, wishing I could reach into her brain and shake it, convince her that women could be more than just submissive daughters and wives if they chose, that they were fully equal to men and she was wasting herself out here in these fields. But I felt so helpless and weak against her convictions.

"But, Abigail—"

"That's what I believe," she said, looking at me, no expression on her face. "It's not up to you."

"Girls!" called Mrs. Dean from the porch. "Time to come in and get dinner ready! Where are you?"

"Here, Mama," Abigail said, standing up.

"What were you doing sitting in the garden? Come on up here and get yourself cleaned up! It's a big night!"

As I got up, Abigail stopped and turned toward me. "Remember what I asked," she said.

"Right, telling Asher," I said.

She nodded.

"And after I do that," I said, taking a deep breath to steady myself, "I'll leave. Tomorrow."

Abigail looked surprised and sad for a moment, but then she closed her eyes and nodded. "That's probably a good idea."

TWENTY-TWO

While Abigail, Mrs. Dean, and I toiled in the kitchen (I'd been given the task of cutting up vegetables for the salad, which even I couldn't screw up), Beau and Mr. Dean were secluded in the study.

We were all throwing anxious glances over at the closed door, wondering what was going on inside. Mrs. Dean would giggle occasionally and give her daughter a little hip bump. Abigail would smile back with clear and delighted eyes.

I had to give it to her, Abigail was a far better actress than I could ever be. If I didn't know better, I would have thought she was actually happy.

"So exciting!" Mrs. Dean said in her just-us-girls voice, which now made me feel a bit sick given the circumstances. "My little princess is growing up!"

"Mama, hush," said Abigail. "We don't know what they're talking about in there."

"A little bird told me it's a very, very important conversation," said Mrs. Dean.

Chastity, who was setting the table, put down the last plate so hard I was surprised it didn't break. "What *is* it, Mama?" she said. "Why won't anyone tell me what's going on?"

"Be gentle! You'll find out soon enough, munchkin." Mrs. Dean turned back toward the stove. She started humming.

Chastity watched her, looking as if she might burst into tears. I suddenly realized that if Abigail got married and left, Chastity, as the next-oldest daughter, would move into the spot of eldest at-home daughter and take over all the tasks that position entailed. Even though she was just fourteen, it would be the end of her childhood. Obviously she'd figured that out.

Chastity noticed I was watching and looked at me with watery eyes. I smiled at her, but she just sighed and turned away.

I went back to cutting the vegetables and tried to enjoy the noise of a large family surrounding me. I'd looked up bus times online, bought a ticket, and told Abigail that I would leave tomorrow morning. But beyond all the embarrassment I'd just endured, I was sad that this was my last night with the Dean family. My last night to take it all in.

Despite everything, despite the fact I found so many of their beliefs deeply upsetting and wished I could snatch

Abigail and Asher up and take them back to Chicago with me so they could be normal teenagers, I'd miss this place. The chaos of all the little kids, the baby girl who was so sweet and squishy, the constant smell of cooking food, the way everyone worked together and spent so much time around each other with barely any fighting.

My house would be the same—quiet and dark and mostly empty. My parents always gone. My brother a stranger.

I sighed and looked down at the cutting board. At least I'd learned to slice carrots into neat little chunks. Maybe I could apply some other lessons to my life.

The men emerged from the study a few minutes later, looking pleased with themselves, like they'd just conducted a successful business meeting. And I remembered why I would be happy to leave.

. . .

I sat directly across the table from Beau and made it my mission to give him as many dirty looks as possible.

He'd be in the middle of bragging about something and his eyes would sweep over the table to assess the audience and there I would be, shooting daggers directly into his skull.

Once, he laughed nervously and smiled at me. "Everything okay there, Faithy? You look a little peaked."

The rest of the table turned to stare at me. Abigail in particular gave me an exasperated look. "Oh, I'm fine," I said. "It's just…you have something gross in your teeth. Right there."

I knew that would bother a fastidious guy like Beau, with his carefully slicked hair that reminded me of Blake once I'd made the connection. He picked at his mouth anxiously and bared his teeth to everyone. "Is it gone?"

I glanced over at Mr. Dean, who was openly glaring at me. "Well, now, that's not very polite is it?" he said. He tried to laugh jovially, but it came out fake and forced.

"Mama, Daddy," Abigail said, in an obvious attempt to diffuse tension, "Faith's mother called today and it turns out she really wants her home sooner than planned. So Faith is leaving tomorrow on the bus. This will be her last night here."

"Oh no!" said Mrs. Dean. The little kids sang a chorus of "Don't go!" Asher looked wide-eyed down at his plate and wouldn't even meet my glance.

"Why does she need you back?" Mrs. Dean asked, pouting. "We so wanted to keep you forever!"

"Um," I said, my mind blank, and Abigail nudged me under the table. "She needs me home to help out because she's…um…sick."

"Oh dear," said Mrs. Dean. "That's terrible!"

"I'm sure she'll be okay, she just misses me," I said in a rush. I slowly raised my eyes to look at Asher. He was still staring down at his plate, and my stomach sunk. I still had a lot of explaining to do tonight.

"That's all too bad," said Mr. Dean. "But we will pray for your safe travels, Faith. Won't we, children?"

"Yes, Daddy," they all replied dutifully.

"But I'm sure Abigail will be glad to have you, her dear friend, here tonight," continued Mr. Dean. "Because it turns out this is the most important night of her life."

We all turned to look at Abigail, whose eyes went wide. "It ... is?"

"Yes, child. Because this fine gentleman right here," he said, indicating Beau, who assumed a smarmy smile as we all turned to look at him instead, "has just requested to be given your hand in courtship. And I, after some consideration, have given him my permission."

"How wonderful!" burst out Mrs. Dean, and then clapped her hands to her mouth when Mr. Dean gave her a stern look. "Sorry, Daddy, I didn't mean to interrupt."

"It's okay, Mama, it is a wonderful occasion," he said with a smile. Then he looked at Abigail. "What do you say to that, girl?"

I looked over at Abigail, whose face was so tense I could almost see the muscles in her mouth quivering. I noticed she hadn't eaten any of her food.

"That's ... that's really amazing. I don't even know what to say," she said. Each word appeared to take so much effort, I was surprised she didn't burst apart. "Praise God. I'm so happy, Daddy."

All of the kids around the table erupted into excited whispers.

"Does that mean they're gonna get married and have a baby?" asked Luke loudly. "Like Elijah and Rachel?"

"That's what I hope for, of course," said Beau, in such a self-satisfied tone that I wanted to throw my plate at him.

I was still watching Abigail. She glanced over at Beau and smiled demurely, and he grinned back at her.

"What do you say, Abigail?" he said. "Shall we pray over it together and see where the Lord leads us?"

"Only if you have an escort to make sure there are no shenanigans!" sang Mrs. Dean, looking around at the little kids. "Fortunately, we have lots of good little escorts here, don't we?"

The children all smiled and wiggled in their seats, familiar with the procedure. Even if Beau and Abigail were practically engaged, it didn't mean they could be alone yet.

"How about we go sit on the front porch, darling?" said Beau. "We'll have ourselves a little prayer and a talk."

"Okay, whatever you'd like to do, Beau," said Abigail softly, in a submissive voice that broke my heart on the spot.

She had completely given up.

TWENTY-THREE

Since Abigail was out on the porch with Beau and Chastity, who was acting as the first escort, Asher helped his mom and me clear the table.

"Isn't that sweet, a man helping out around the house? Asher's always been so good at that," simpered his mom. "Faith, you need to find yourself a good boy like this one!"

She ruffled his hair and walked away. Asher rolled his eyes and gave me a small smile.

"You're really leaving so quick?" he murmured, when Mrs. Dean was far enough away not to hear.

"Yes, and I need to talk to you before I go," I whispered back.

"Okay. The barn, after prayers," he replied, and walked away with a stack of dirty dishes.

The hours ticked slowly by. Abigail and Beau came back inside, holding hands, the first time they were officially allowed to touch each other. Beau was strutting proudly, like he'd won a prize at the fair. And Abigail looked quietly defeated, her shoulders hunched a little, even as she smiled. They sat next to each other on a love seat during prayers, as the younger kids took turns staring at them to make sure there wasn't any funny business. It would have been sweet and comical if it weren't so … gross.

Mr. Dean said a long prayer for the courting couple, asking for the Heavenly Father to send wisdom to their hearts as they embarked on their new path together. I sat and silently seethed, wondering what Jesus would really think of a man who cornered a teenaged girl in a barn and molested her and got away with it.

Not only got away with it, but then managed to get engaged to her, convincing her that's what she'd wanted all along. That she had asked for it.

It was so upsetting that I had to block it all out and concentrate on more pleasant things. Such as watching Asher as surreptitiously as possible. Occasionally he glanced back at me, and our eyes would meet for a second like a swift electric shock.

My mind drifted away from the prayers as I thought about how he might react to the truth about me. I dreamed of a best-case scenario in which he gave up his fanatical family and moved to Chicago to go to college. And then we could date like normal people and hang out and do couple-y things and thereby make my senior year of high school livable.

But who was I kidding? When he found out, he would

think I was a horrible selfish lying jerk, and it would be the truth. Even my best-case scenario was selfish, because it involved him abandoning his family and home and beliefs and everything he'd ever known. And all for what? Me? Like that was worth it?

The best thing I could do was just go away and leave him in peace.

I decided I shouldn't hope for much. Any end result in which he didn't end up hating my guts would have to be good enough.

. . .

When the final evening-prayer amens were said and everyone was milling around before bed, I saw Asher slip out the back door. After a few minutes, I followed him, running silently across the dewy backyard on bare feet.

He was standing where we'd first kissed, leaning against the back of the barn and watching the sky, arms crossed against his chest.

"Asher," I said softly, and he turned. Without a word, he walked up and took me in his arms, hugging me against him. After my surprise wore off, I put my arms around him too, and for a minute we were just two nameless people under the stars, standing so close it was like we were a single unit.

"I'm sorry," he said. "I can't say anything to Dad about Beau. Not now that Abigail told me not to. Not now that it's official. It's what she wants. It wouldn't make a difference."

I swallowed hard. "I know. I just wish it weren't true."

He moved his face down the side of my head and took a deep breath.

"But I'm glad that you told me. And I hate that you're leaving," he said into my hair. "Is it because Abigail's angry that you told me?"

"Yes," I said, already feeling choked up. He smelled like fresh-cut grass and clean boy, and I inhaled deeply, wishing I could somehow bottle that scent up and save it for later. When I was alone again.

"I'll miss you so much, Faith," he said. "You're not like any girl I've ever met before."

"Really?" I said, soaking up the last few moments before I'd have to tell him the truth and make him hate me.

"You're the only girl I know who makes me feel ... normal."

"I know exactly what you mean," I said.

I closed my eyes against his chest, hugging him harder and wishing I actually was Faith. Because maybe that way I could see him again, and maybe we could both help each other feel normal and loved. It felt so unfair.

This is all my fault, I thought. *It's my fault and I have to make it right.*

With a grimace, I pushed away from him, wiping my eyes. I stumbled a few feet farther away until I was almost outside of the circle of the barn light, far enough away so I couldn't smell him anymore.

"Faith?" he said worriedly.

"Asher, I have to tell you something," I said in a shaking voice. I stopped, trying to collect myself.

"What?"

"I ... I don't even know how to say this."

He came up behind me and put his big hands on my shoulders. "Start at the beginning?" he suggested. "Whatever it is can't be that bad."

I took a deep breath. Then another. Then one more for good measure. The oxygen started to make me feel a little lightheaded.

"My name isn't Faith," I said in a rush. "My name is Dylan and I'm from a suburb of Chicago and I honestly don't even know if I believe in God. I lied about all of that. I pretended to be Faith because I got a little ... well ... obsessed with your family and religion and Abigail's blog and we became friends and when she invited me to visit because she thought I was Faith, I came because I wanted to see it for myself."

His hands went slack. Then they were gone.

I turned around to look at his face, which was blank and staring at some unseen point out in the darkness of the field. His arms hung down by his sides.

"But, Asher, even though I lied about my name and, um, all those other things, I didn't lie about me," I said, heart racing. "I mean, this is who I am, this person in front of you who's talking to you right now. I'm not some amazing actress ... I wasn't faking my personality or anything. Well, not most of it. And I really do like you and think you're sweet and awesome and completely and totally normal. I mean, *I* do, as Dylan. I really, really like you."

He continued staring blankly.

I gave him a few more seconds. "Asher? Will you ... will you please say something?"

For the first time, he looked at me. Like he was surprised I was still there.

"Wh-wh-what am I supposed to say?" he asked, his voice scratchy.

"I don't know," I admitted. "Whatever you're feeling. Go ahead and throw it at me. I can take it."

He cocked his head to the side, as if processing, and after a few more moments, he asked, "Does Abigail know?"

"Yes," I admitted. "She sort of ... found out. My mom called my cell phone and Abigail picked it up. She figured it out from there."

"So your parents didn't know you were here?"

"No," I said. "They think I'm at a camp. In Springfield."

"Oh."

He went back to leaning against the hay bales. I followed him at a distance, giving him some space.

"Don't you have anything else to say?" I asked after a few moments.

He looked at me and shrugged. "You know, I guess it all makes sense."

"What makes sense?"

He shrugged again. "Why you are the way you are."

"How am I?"

He almost cracked a smile. "Unconcerned with ... you know, all the cussing. For example."

"It's true. I have kind of a dirty mouth sometimes," I said, giving him a small smile back.

"And the kissing," he said.

I gave an embarrassed shrug. "I kind of like kissing. And I'm sorry if that freaked you out. I feel like maybe I pushed you."

Asher actually laughed. "Um, it wasn't anything I didn't want too," he pointed out. "I pushed you, too."

But then he pursed his lips together, looking disturbed.

"So have you ... have you had boyfriends before?" he asked.

I nodded, reluctantly, wishing I didn't have to count a terrible boyfriend like Blake. "Just one. Barely."

"Oh," he said, looking down at the ground.

"See, well, people do that where I live," I said. "Have boyfriends and girlfriends and hook up and things. It's not like—"

"I know that," he said shortly. "You think I don't know that? I've seen stuff like that ... I mean, at least a little bit."

"Right. Abigail told me about your girlfriend," I said. "How your dad made you break up with her and quit college."

Asher hugged his arms around his chest. "Yeah. I figured she told you about that."

"So ... do you still love that girl?" I asked, cringing off into the darkness as I waited for a reply.

"No," he said with a sigh. "I saw her in town a few

weeks ago. She was holding hands with another guy. She looked happy. Not that I can blame her or anything. I'm no good for anyone. Too much of a weirdo, especially for a girl who's ... normal."

That made my heart hurt. "Asher, you're not a weirdo. You just want to be close to someone. That's not strange at all."

"I should only want to be with my wife," he said. "That's what I've been told my whole life, anyway."

"Oh, so you can end up like Abigail and Beau in there? Get yourself trapped in something when you're too young to know what you actually want? Maybe get married to someone you don't even like that much, just because your fathers believe the same thing?"

I could hear my voice heating up, so angry for Abigail and Asher and the rigid roles they'd been raised to fill. And at the fact that they acted like they had absolutely no choice in the matter, even if they did. They just let it happen to them, like they were passive players in their own lives.

Asher cringed at my tone. "I don't know. I don't know what I think anymore. I saw how people lived out in the world and sometimes ... sometimes I just want to leave this house. So badly it hurts. Just take off and change my name and never look back. But ... they're my family. This is where I'm from. And these things that they believe, about how we know the truth and the rest of the world is wrong and sinful ... I mean, that's how I've been raised. That's in my brain."

"But people don't always end up believing exactly

what their parents taught them," I said. "Everyone has free will to—"

"It's not a faucet I can turn off," Asher interrupted. "It's not a button I can push when I decide I'm done believing. It's my *faith*."

I stayed silent, biting my lip. I had no idea what to say to him, afraid that if I said too much of what I really thought, like I'd done with Abigail, he would just shut down and dismiss me. And who was I to declare that his faith was wrong?

"So tell me about him," Asher said.

"Who?"

"Your boyfriend. What's his name?"

"Well, he's very much my *ex*-boyfriend. And his name was Blake."

"*Blake*," Asher said, like it was a bad word.

"He wasn't the nicest guy," I admitted. "Actually, he's basically your polar opposite."

"Oh?" said Asher, giving me a half smile. "How's that?"

"He's selfish and cruel," I said. "He uses people ... well, in particular he uses girls ... and never feels bad about it."

He ruined my life, I wanted to say. But then Asher would ask why, and I'd have to tell him about the pictures. And things were going so shockingly well that I couldn't end it yet. Even though I knew he'd eventually find out the truth.

"Why did you ever go out with him, then?" asked Asher.

I shrugged. "He's really cute and popular and I'm ... not. And in my school, that's not something you really turn down, you know? Someone higher up on the social scale deciding they like you, or whatever. Or at least I couldn't turn it down at the time. I ... I guess I wasn't strong enough. I was basically willing to give up everything for him."

"Are you strong enough now?"

I thought over the past dark months of my life, when it felt like I didn't have a friend in the world and that it was all my fault. Scuttling through the halls and hiding in my room, attached to my computer where I pretended to be someone completely different. Would I be strong enough to walk away from someone like Blake now? Someone who swept in with manipulative words and smiles and tried to take over my life?

I looked over at Asher. "I think I would be. At least, I hope so."

He put his arm around me and drew me close, which completely surprised me. He knew most of my terrible lies, and he still wanted to touch me.

"I think you know for sure, Faith," he said, his warm hand running up and down my spine like he was bracing me.

"Dylan," I corrected.

"I mean, I think you know, Dylan," he said, with a small laugh. "I think you're better and stronger than that. I think you're amazing."

I leaned my head against his chest, listening to his heartbeat and savoring the moment. It was maybe the last moment I'd ever have with him.

Because then a harsh voice broke the darkness.

"Well. Just what is going on here?"

It was Mr. Dean.

TWENTY-FOUR

Asher and I both froze in terror.

"Son, what are you doing laying hands on that girl?" Mr. Dean asked, his voice shaking.

We stepped away from each other quickly and looked at Mr. Dean. Even in the dim barn light, I could tell that his face was bright red with anger.

"She ... uh ... uh ... " Asher's stutter seemed to act up under stress.

"*Uh uh uh,*" Mr. Dean said mockingly. "Speak up like a man, please!"

I watched Asher's shoulders slump and he pursed his lips together.

"I was upset about leaving," I said, trying not to sound too confrontational. "Asher was just being nice and comforting me."

Mr. Dean turned on me, looking so hostile that I took a

step back. "When I want to hear you speak, little girl, I'll ask you to say something. Otherwise, just shut your mouth!"

I felt myself shrink, stunned from being talked to so harshly. It felt like the bullies at school. It felt like Blake.

"Don't talk to her like that," Asher said.

Mr. Dean turned on him. "What did you just say?"

"I said, don't talk to her like that," Asher replied. "Sir."

"So you're in charge around here now, telling people how they ought to talk? Is that it, Mr. *Uh Uh Uh*?" taunted Mr. Dean.

Asher started to look panicky, his face reddening like his father's.

"That's what I thought," said Mr. Dean. "You have no guts to back up what you say. Always took after your mother's side, a bunch of weaklings. So, what, you still think you're some sort of Casanova out here, sinning with this poor little girl? After what happened the last time? Haven't you learned anything, boy?"

God, I hated the way he dismissed me like that, like I was a small child. Like I didn't count for anything.

"Mr. Dean," I said. "Please don't blame Asher. It was all my fault. I was out here and—"

"WHAT DID I SAY BEFORE?" he yelled, and I took another step back. I was crushed against the barn wall now. "Your father must not have a very good hold on you, if you go around interrupting men when they're talking!"

I wanted to leave, to get away from this black hole of anger, but I couldn't abandon Asher to face him alone.

"Dad, I want you to stop yelling at her," Asher said firmly. "Right now."

Mr. Dean looked at him for a moment, then began to walk forward, his hand raised.

"What did you just say?"

"I...I...I said stop yelling at her," Asher repeated, holding his chin up defiantly. They were the same height.

"That's what I thought you said. Apparently you have forgotten your place." And Mr. Dean slapped him hard, right across the face. Asher spun halfway around, clutching at his cheek, silent.

I couldn't help it. I let out a cry, clapping my hand over my mouth.

"And if you were under my control, girlie, I'd do the same to you," Mr. Dean said to me. "It's a good thing you're leaving tomorrow, because you're trying my patience. Now both of you, get yourselves inside. I will not stand another minute of this rebellion."

I watched Asher, my fists clenched, hoping he wouldn't follow his father's commands. Hoping he would stand on the spot and tell Mr. Dean to go to hell.

But, without looking in my direction, Asher started walking toward the house.

"Asher?" I called after him.

Mr. Dean grabbed my upper arm, his fingers steely. "Get moving, miss," he said.

I glared at him and shook my arm out of his grip. "Don't touch me, you creep," I said. "Or my mom will sue you."

Maybe his kids were afraid of him, but I wasn't going

to let a controlling old woman-hater like Mr. Dean tell me what to do.

Mr. Dean looked surprised at my sass, but I didn't stick around to see what he'd do next.

I ran to catch up with Asher, who was already halfway to the door.

"Asher, listen, you don't need to—"

He turned toward me swiftly, his eyes hard and full of tears.

"Please don't make it worse for me," he whispered. His cheek was puffy and all I wanted was to put my hand on it.

"But you know that you can leave at any—"

"Please, Dylan," he said softly. "I'm not strong like you."

As Mr. Dean stalked up, Asher held the screen door open, politely. "After you, Faith."

. . .

Abigail was lying propped up in bed reading her Bible when I got to her room. I could see that she'd been crying; there was a box of tissues on the bed next to her.

I sat down on my bed, trying to calm my racing heart.

She took a deep breath that was really more of a prolonged sniffle and looked at me. "So, did you tell Asher?"

I nodded.

"And? How did he take it?"

"Surprisingly well, I guess, considering," I replied.

She laughed a little. "That's Asher. So willing to forgive. I told you that he really adored you."

I shrugged, embarrassed and unwilling to show I believed that one way or the other.

"But we didn't get to talk for very long and there was a lot more to say," I said. "Your dad found us out there. While we were, um, hugging."

"Wow," she said, her eyes wide, shutting her Bible and putting it on the bedside table. "I'm sure that didn't go over well."

"Nope. It's probably a good thing I'm leaving tomorrow. For a variety of reasons."

"Yes, I suppose it is," she replied with tiny smile. "But, you know, if the Lord wants you and Asher to be together, then..."

"Right," I said. "If it's meant to be, it'll somehow happen, I guess."

We sat in silence for a minute, lost in our own heads. I thought about what I could say to this girl who suddenly knew me so well. Even some of the deep, dark layers of me that I'd tried to hide from her for all these months. And I knew some of her deep, dark layers too.

"So, I guess I should tell you congratulations," I said.

Abigail closed her eyes. "Don't."

"But isn't that what people say when other people get engaged?"

"I already know what you think," she said. "You don't have to act like you're thinking anything else. And we're not engaged yet, anyway... it's a courtship."

I rolled my eyes as I stood up to start changing into

that hideous nightgown for the last time. She was full of it, trying to downplay the significance of what was happening.

"I don't suppose there's anything at all I could say that would change your mind?" I asked, yanking the nightgown over my head so hard that some of the seams crackled.

"No," she said.

I sat down on my bed, feeling frustration bubbling over in me, urging me to say inflammatory, hurtful things.

"What if I told you about my real life back home, where I don't have to cook and clean and I'm free to do whatever I want, up to and including *not* getting married to some jerk and becoming his broodmare when I'm eighteen? And about how someday I'll have a career, hopefully doing something I enjoy, that I'll contribute to the world. And maybe I'll get married and have kids or maybe I won't, but it will be my choice about when that happens and under what circumstances."

I knew I was just being cruel, but now that everything was out in the open, I couldn't stop myself from going at it with every weapon at my disposal.

Abigail closed her eyes even tighter, scrunching her nose. "No," she said. "That doesn't change anything."

I sighed and looked at her. "How about if I tell you that I think you're meant for so much more, Abigail," I said, feeling like I might start to cry soon. Either cry or punch through a wall with my bare fists. "How you're smart and funny and beautiful and you care about people, and you're way too good to just get tied down, this young, to a jerk like Beau. You're too good for this whole stupid place."

"'Charm is deceitful, and beauty is vain, but a woman who fears the Lord is to be praised,'" she said, her eyes still closed, as if looking at me would give my words some validity.

I took a deep breath, held it for a moment, and then let it out. And I knew I had to stop.

Abigail had made her choice, and there was nothing else I could say to try and convince her. As much as I wanted her to jump up and suddenly proclaim that she'd changed her mind, that she wasn't going to let her life happen to her, that she was going to fight, I knew she wouldn't.

So I got underneath the covers and then reached over to turn off the lamp.

I lay there and breathed for moment, calming myself.

"Okay, one last thing," I said, and heard her sigh in exasperation. "Just one thing and then I'll shut up, I promise."

"Fine," she said. "What?"

"If you ever need help—if you ever need to get away somewhere and you feel like your family wouldn't understand or let you come back here—even if you just need to take a little break," I said, "you can call me. Anytime. Day or night, I don't care if it's ten years from now. Whatever the circumstances. And I will come get you."

There was a long moment of silence, and I began to think she was just going to ignore me. Maybe she was thinking about how if she were in trouble, the absolute last thing she'd do is call on some crazy girl who'd lied her way into the Dean household and whose naked pictures were plastered all over the Internet.

But then I heard her take a shaky breath.

"Thank you, Dylan," she said in a small voice. "I'll remember that."

TWENTY-FIVE

I was packed and ready to go early the next morning. I felt like I'd come to terms with the situation, and that as long as I could say one last goodbye to Asher, I would be okay with leaving.

But when I went down to breakfast, Asher wasn't there.

As I helped Mrs. Dean cook eggs for the last time, she gave me a little nudge with her hip.

"Daddy told me about what happened last night with you and Asher over by the barn," she whispered. "Don't you worry, Daddy's all bark and no bite. And I'm sure he was just mistaken about what was going on."

Maybe Mr. Dean had omitted the fact that he'd hit Asher when recounting the story to his wife. Since that would definitely qualify as a bite.

"Oh," was all I could think of to say. "Okay."

"I'm afraid we made some mistakes while we were

raising that boy. He was just such a willful child," Mrs. Dean continued in a low voice. "And he doesn't quite have a handle yet on how to be an honorable man. I'm very sorry if he took advantage of you in any way, Faith, and I hope you won't think badly of us when you leave."

I blinked at her, stung on Asher's behalf.

"He didn't take advantage of me," I said. "Whatever happened wasn't solely his fault. I like him a lot and think he's a great guy. I had as much to do with what happened as he did."

Mrs. Dean turned to look at me with a shocked expression. "Well, goodness! Perhaps it's a good thing you're leaving, then. Although it wouldn't matter anyway, since Daddy took Asher away early this morning."

I dropped the spatula I was holding onto the stove and eggs splattered.

"What? Away? To where?"

Mrs. Dean looked at the stove with an annoyed expression, dabbing with a towel at the mess I'd made. "To stay with some of our family in Georgia. They have a job for him down there on their farm and he can work hard and reflect on his sins," she said. "We should have done it long ago. He needs to get his head straight, Faith. As do you, it seems."

"But … " I said. I couldn't believe I wouldn't get a chance to see Asher one last time, that my last memory of him would be his dad hitting him, that we wouldn't have a chance to process what had happened between us. I didn't even have a phone number or an email address for him.

How could it just end like this?

Mrs. Dean shoved some plates at me. "It's all in the past now, praise God!" she said in her little girl voice.

. . .

After breakfast, I said goodbye to all the little Deans. They crowded around me and looked up with solemn faces, while Abigail and Chastity watched with their arms linked.

"You're the funnest teacher we've ever had," said Jed, and I laughed.

"But I didn't teach you anything!" I said, ruffling his hair and irrationally wishing I could take them all with me. Just load up the whole Dean brood and install them in my basement back home. "You guys taught *me* a lot more, you know."

"Still," Jed said, and sighed. "It was fun having someone new around. We never meet anyone new."

. . .

Mrs. Dean drove Abigail and me into town so I could catch the bus.

I craned my neck around for one last look at the farmhouse. I couldn't believe it had been barely ten days since I'd first seen it, riding in the truck with Abigail and Asher, experiencing the dawning realization of what I'd gotten myself into. It felt like years since then.

"I'm sure your mother will be happy to have you home," Mrs. Dean said cheerfully. As I expected, she'd simply glossed over our interaction in the kitchen earlier, as if it had never happened. "You must be such a nice little helper to her."

I thought about my house, how cool and dark it was and how rarely my mom was even there. I thought of Scottie always in his room, and Dad always down in his man-cave in the basement. How even when we went on vacation together, we always ended up doing our own separate things. Sometimes it just felt like we were strangers thrown into the same family.

Despite the many faults of the Dean family, I had to admit they did do some things so much better than my own family. They ate together, and talked to each other, and spent nearly all day working alongside each other. At the very least, all the Dean kids knew what their parents believed and what was expected. While so much of the time, with all my freedom, I felt lost.

Someday, I thought, *when I have a family of my own, I'm going to try and do it better than any of them.*

"I try to be a good helper," I said to Mrs. Dean. "But I might not be as big of a help as I could be. It's hard sometimes."

"We all have our trials and shortcomings," she said kindly. "As long as you pray and remain faithful, God will show you what you need to do."

"Right," I said. "Of course."

We were all silent for a few minutes as the car bumped over the rutted gravel road.

"Thank you both for having me," I said. "I've learned so much."

Abigail, who had been quiet the whole way, gave me an incredulous look. "Really?"

"Sure," I said.

"Are you excited to share some stories with your family and friends back home?" she asked, in a slightly pointed tone.

"Maybe," I said. "They'll be interested in hearing about... some of the things. Some of it I'd just like to keep to myself, I guess."

I hoped she understood my meaning—that I didn't intend to go back home and talk about Abigail and her secrets like she'd been an animal in a zoo. That I was going to try and be respectful.

"That's an interesting idea," Abigail said.

Mrs. Dean laughed. "You girlies sound like you're talking in code! Heavens, won't you miss each other so much?"

"Yes," I said honestly. "I hope that Abigail can come visit me sometime."

"Oh, how nice!" Mrs. Dean said.

"Well, of course, I have a busy season ahead of me," Abigail said, picking at her skirt. "With, you know, the courting and all. There won't be much of a chance to get away."

"I know," I said. "But I still hope."

She met my eye for a moment, and then looked out the front window.

We were driving through town now, nearing the intersection where the bus stopped. Mrs. Dean pulled over to the curb and turned to give me a short hug across Abigail's lap.

"Be good, Faith dear. We'll pray for your safe travels."

"Thanks, Mrs. Dean," I said. "You've been very nice to me."

Abigail and I got out of the car and she stood there, her arms crossed tightly against her chest. She gave me an anxious look, seeming almost near tears. Her face was splotchy. It was so different from the first time I'd seen her, bouncing and happy, that I felt like my presence might have ruined everything.

"I guess this is it," I said, setting my bag down on the ground.

"I guess so," she said, and then furrowed her eyebrows. "I can't figure out why it is that I think I'm going to miss you."

"My winning personality and charming sense of humor, obviously," I said, grinning.

"It's true. I guess you can be pretty funny." She gave me a small answering smile. "Are you going to keep blogging?"

I thought about it for a moment. "I don't think so. I don't know. Honestly, I'm kind of confused about the whole thing."

Abigail nodded, biting her lip. "It was kind of devious for you to lie on your site and make all that up," she said. "But... you do have a knack with words, I'll give you that. I mean, *I* totally believed you."

I found this compliment to be far more thrilling than was really appropriate for the moment.

"Thanks," I said. "For what it's worth, I really am sorry I lied to you."

"You are?" she asked.

I nodded.

"Then please shut your site down," she said. "It's just ... not a good thing to do. You know that."

I took a deep breath, panicking for a moment about giving up Faith. But then a feeling of certainty overtook me and I knew she was correct. "You're so right, Abigail. It's wrong. I promise I'll shut it down." I paused, then smiled. "You might think I'm awful for saying this, but I don't actually regret making it."

"Oh?" she asked. "Even after all this?"

"No. Because I got to meet you. And Asher."

"I have to say, you didn't exactly improve our lives much," she said with a laugh. "You basically just came in and shook everything up like a snow globe. I'm not even sure how it'll all settle down again."

Maybe that's not a bad thing, I wanted to say. But I didn't. Abigail already knew I thought that.

I stepped forward and put my arms around her. She allowed me to hug her, but kept her arms crossed between us and didn't reciprocate. When I pulled away I could see that her eyes were damp. Then she reached into her skirt pocket and pulled out a folded piece of paper.

"He left this for you," she said, handing it over. And she turned away to go to the car door.

I looked at the piece of paper, confused. "Oh ... thanks."

Abigail turned back toward me once more and smiled dimly. "I'll pray for you, Dylan. I'll hope that you find your way."

"Bye, Abigail," I said. "I hope the same. For both of us."

As their car drove away, I opened the paper with trembling fingers.

It was a short message, written in pencil, obviously dashed off in a hurry.

Dylan,

As soon as I deserve you, I will come and find you.

Love, Asher

TWENTY-SIX

I spent the first hour of the bus ride home in a sort of daze, my eyes closed, trying to transition my brain back into being Dylan again.

Then I took out Asher's note, and it hit me and rolled over me like a tidal wave, all of the things that had happened in the past ten days. And the fact that it was over.

There had been such amazing highs. Finally feeling like I had a friend again, in Abigail—someone who judged me for who I was in the present, not for what I'd done in my previous life. And finally meeting a boy who didn't scare me and make me clam up like a fool, who held me in just the right way and who I felt like I could trust.

And then there were the awful lows, the things that kept replaying in my brain like an inescapable horror movie. Being called out as a liar by Abigail and having to explain myself had been horrible and embarrassing, but nothing matched the squirmy wretchedness I felt watching her bind herself to Beau.

Or how horrifying it was to see Asher get hit by his dad. Because of me.

Or the way all of those kids were trapped in that house, thinking they had no other options. That they were making their God happy by living apart and being ignorant of the rest of the world.

I turned Asher's folded note around and around in my hand, even put it up to my lips for a moment, willing myself not to cry. I didn't know where to go from here.

. . .

The bus stop was in the middle of downtown Chicago, in a dense corporate area of towering buildings. I stepped off just as rush hour was beginning. Thousands of people in dark business clothes were crowding the sidewalks and rushing to catch trains back to their homes in the suburbs. I felt like a strange exclamation point walking among them in my long denim skirt and unstylish pink blouse. I caught people giving me sideways glances, as if trying to figure out my place in this bustling city.

After ten days on a relatively quiet farm, the noise and crush was almost overwhelming.

But eventually I got to the Metra train that would take me home. I sat next to a kind-faced woman in a red suit and bright white commuter tennis shoes. She talked quietly on her cell phone, asking the person on the other end what they were fixing for dinner.

I couldn't help but smile. It felt like my perspective shifted. Here was normal.

As I walked the long mile from the train station to my house, I considered explanations for why I was home a few days earlier than expected. I predicted that my parents would freak out and think that I'd been thrown out of camp for bad behavior or something. But I knew that nothing worked better or more efficiently than telling the actual truth.

And I was tired of hiding and lying.

All my confidence flooded out of me, though, when I saw my mom's car in the driveway. She shouldn't have been home at that hour—it was way too early. I'd expected to have more time than this to prepare, or at least time to change clothes, but apparently I would have to face the situation immediately.

I let myself in and stood in the entryway. From somewhere upstairs, there was rock music playing. Weird.

I took a deep breath.

"Mom?" I called.

After a second, the music switched off. "Who's there?" my mom's voice called back.

"Mom, it's me," I said, putting down my bag and walking up the stairs.

She emerged from the upstairs hallway, dressed in ratty jeans and an old button-down shirt of my dad's. Her hair was pulled back in a messy half ponytail and there were smudges of lavender paint on her hands and her face.

"Dylan! What are you doing back? I called you the other day and you never called back!" she said as I climbed the stairs to reach her. "And ... and what the hell are you wearing?"

She grabbed me by the shoulders and gave my outfit an incredulous once-over. "Is this the style these days? God, I'm so out of it."

There was something so strangely bright about her. So free and gleeful. And I was overcome with missing her, even though she was right there in front of me.

I threw my arms around her shoulders. "I missed you, Mom."

She hugged me back, seeming surprised. "I missed you too, Pickle! How was it? Did you learn a lot?"

"Yes," I said, still clinging to her, feeling tearful again.

She drew back and looked into my face. "Are you okay?"

I nodded, pressing my palms to the corners of my eyes. "Just kind of emotional right now, I guess. You know."

"Well, maybe this will make you feel better," she said, walking off down the hallway. "I thought I had a few more days to get it done, but now you can help me finish up."

I followed her down the hall to my room, where all of my furniture was pushed into the middle of the floor and covered with plastic. On my dresser were a CD player and a glass of white wine.

The dark blue walls of my bedroom, the ones I'd

painted myself when I was fourteen, were in the process of becoming a light, cheerful purple.

Mom was searching my face.

"I'm sorry, I know I should have asked you first," she said. "But I came up here the other day, just to look in, and I couldn't believe how *dark* and claustrophobic this room was. It felt like being in a cave or drowning underwater. So I thought I'd surprise you. Do you like the color? If not, we can paint it something else, but I just thought this was so pretty."

It felt like a whole new happy planet in there. I looked at her and slowly nodded.

She put her arm over my shoulders. "Good! Well, that's a relief."

"But ... how do you have time to do this?" I asked. "And why are you even home?"

"Oh, I didn't tell you yet!" she said. "I took myself off the arbitration."

"You ... what?" I said, confused.

"Took myself off," she repeated. "I gave it to some of the younger associates. The client was being ridiculous and it's been three damn years and I'd been doing a lot of thinking the past few months about how I want to live and what I should prioritize. And it just slowly became clear— slaving away on that case was *not* it."

"You ... wait, you gave it away?"

"Yeah! I figured, I'm a partner, I worked my ass off to get there, and why shouldn't I take advantage of my seniority a bit? It seems like all the boys get to take time off for their little midlife crises, and what do I ever get? So I decided I'd take a nice long summer break, and here I am. Drinking wine and painting my daughter's room. It feels fantastic. And now you're back! God, Dylan, we'll have a blast!"

"A...break?" I said. I couldn't process what I was hearing. Mom had been obsessed with that case since I'd started high school. I could barely remember a time when it wasn't a part of all our lives.

"Sure!" she said, and then her face turned solemn. "I've been doing a lot of thinking about how I haven't been here for you as much as you needed me to be, especially this past year with everything that happened. I know I let that damn case take over my life. Even as it was happening, I knew I was allowing it to get out of control. And here you are, only a year away from going off to college, and Scottie is in high school, too, and soon you'll both be grown up and gone forever, and what will I have spent my time on?"

She sighed, and then looked at me and smiled. "I hope I can make it up to you both this summer, at least a little bit. I'm going to make Dad take some time off, too. Bring some balance back to this family. I was wondering...what do you think about taking a kickboxing class with me?"

The lump in my throat grew, until I felt like it might be bigger than my head.

"Does that sound good, Pickle?"

"Sure, Mom. It sounds really great."

I reached over and hugged her again, my badass lawyer mom, so strong and sure of herself. So ready to admit that she'd been wrong and to change and tackle life.

"So, do you want to tell me about this camp you went to?" she asked. "Is this a future state legislator that I'm hugging?"

I laughed. "Maybe!"

"The girl who answered your phone when I called sounded a little strange," she said, pulling back and looking at my face. "What were the people like?"

Instead of answering, I walked over to my dresser and picked up the glass of white wine as if I were going to take a swig.

"Hey, stop that! You're not old enough!" said Mom, scandalized.

Part of me wanted to snort and say *Oh, so now you're all concerned about underage drinking?* But instead of sassing off, I walked over and handed the glass to her. "All right, but *you* might want to finish this off," I said.

Her eyes went wide. "Uh oh. Why?"

In response, I sat down on the plastic tarp on the floor, motioning her to do the same.

"Because I have a lot to tell you."

TWENTY-SEVEN

Mom tried to feign being very displeased and disappointed that I had lied to the Dean family.

"I insist that you write the whole family an apology," she said sternly. "That wasn't very nice of you to do to them. In fact, it was fraud. You took advantage of their trust, Dylan!"

I nodded. "I know."

She scowled at me for a moment, but then softened.

"But ... they ... they really have *courtships*?" she said, a fascinated gleam in her eye. "And girls never get to leave home until they're married? No college at all, ever? What do they think this is—the Dark Ages?"

Mom wanted to know all the gory details—all the things that had also captivated me at the beginning. I began to feel a little guilty relaying them, like I was betraying some confidence to Abigail. So I omitted certain things that felt too private … Abigail's secret about Beau and Mr. Dean hitting Asher among them.

"Wow, Dylan, that's crazy," Mom said, shaking her head and taking a sip of her drink. She'd gone downstairs and gotten us Diet Cokes.

"It's … something," I said, weirdly unwilling to call them crazy now that I'd seen they were real people with feelings and problems and faults. "I mean, in a way, it definitely makes sense. It's safer, I guess."

"The way living in a prison cell is safe?" Mom asked. "Or a sensory deprivation tank?"

I shrugged. "Sort of. But there was just something so … peaceful. I mean, about how they felt like they knew everything. Exactly what God wanted them to do at all times. The exact definition of good. There was nothing to figure out. No reason to be scared about anything. Just read the Bible and it will tell you what to do. Sort of. Though … I guess mostly it was Mr. Dean telling them what to do."

Mom nodded. "I suppose there can be something bizarrely appealing about giving your autonomy over to someone else. It's easier."

I looked at her. It sounded like she got it.

"The world is big and scary, and we're just small people trying to make our way," Mom said. "But, honey, does that really sound like a full life to you? Letting someone else make all the decisions? Letting someone else tell you that you're weak and flawed and need to be taken care of? Letting someone take advantage of you?"

I shook my head. "No."

"You never get to grow up, that way," she said. "You never get to fight it out on your own and figure out who you are. And what you want. And what you can do."

She took a sip of her drink. "Have I ever told you about my favorite time in my whole life? I mean, besides having you and your brother, of course." She patted my leg and winked.

I rolled my eyes. "Whatever."

"It was the two years between undergrad and law school, when I was living in the city in this gross little studio apartment up in Lakeview."

"That sounds cool," I said.

"Cool? I was scared shitless!" Mom replied with a laugh. "It certainly didn't feel cool. My parents were no help at all... they'd already set off for Florida, telling me I'd be fine. But I had no idea who I was, what I wanted. Oh God, I did some of the stupidest things..."

She shook her head, looking off into the distance.

"Like?" I prodded.

"Oh, you know," she said, with a dismissive wave of her hand. "Slept with a few of the wrong kind of guys, got a little too drunk too often. I even almost got arrested once, but that's a story for another time."

"Mom!"

She smiled. "I was terrified and uncertain and inexperienced. And it was only then that I figured out who I really was, and what I really wanted."

I squinted at her.

"To … be a lawyer?" I asked, raising my eyebrow.

"Well, yes, I realized how much I wanted that … professional success. But I also realized that I wanted to be a mom," she said. "And I hoped to someday have a daughter so I could help her fight through that stage of life as well, and convince her that it truly does get better. Because you fight it out, and stumble, and write bad poetry, and pick yourself up again, and at the end, hopefully, someday you're sitting with your kid on her bedroom floor, talking about how you screwed everything up too. Because we all screw up. The test is what we do afterwards."

I smiled at her. She smiled back, reaching over and cupping my cheek.

"And you know, I recently realized how much I was screwing up and not sticking to what I wanted and what I'd planned for myself," she said. "Because I didn't want to be spending my entire life in some skyscraper with a bunch of grumpy clients. I also needed to be with my beautiful, fascinating, brilliant, brave daughter before she grew up and left. And now … how lucky am I? I get to do just that."

I felt like I was looking at my mom for the first time.

"Can I be like you when I grow up?" I asked.

. . .

Mom wanted me to tell Dad and Scottie the whole story, too.

"It's just too good to keep to yourself, you know," she

said when we heard them come home. "You should write a book about it! You know, with names changed and all."

"Maybe," I said, thinking of all the effort I put into Faith's website. "I do like to research and write about stuff I'm interested in, I guess. But I don't know what to do with it. I don't know if that's what I'm meant for. Maybe I could be an investigative journalist? Maybe we could look at colleges that have good journalism programs?"

I glanced at her anxiously, realizing how much I wanted her approval of some identity I hadn't even discovered yet. I wanted to know she hadn't totally given up on me achieving something, even though I'd screwed up so badly.

But Mom's new attitude seemed to extend to the college expectations, too. "Sure, if you want, we can look into it," she said, getting up. "But Dylan, honey, there's absolutely no rush to figure it out right away."

"But you've always been so obsessed with it," I said, confused. I scrambled to my feet to follow her downstairs. "Grades and applications and success and stuff, I mean. Sometimes it sort of seemed like ... like that was all that mattered to you."

Mom stopped in the doorway of my room and turned. She walked up to me and put her hands on my shoulders.

"I know," she said. "But it's not. And I'm sorry if that's the impression I gave you. I was too wrapped up in myself, I guess, and my definition of success. But what's most important is for you to live."

I gave her a dubious look, not sure if I completely trusted this turnaround. Or if I completely liked it. There was something comforting in having parents who expected something out of you.

Mom seemed to realize that maybe she'd gone a little far. She shrugged. "And going to a good college wouldn't hurt, either," she said with a smile. "And for that, of course, you need a good GPA and all..."

That was more like it. "God, Mom, it's summer. Get off my back." I made a face and crossed my arms in a pretend huff.

We both laughed and linked arms to go greet the rest of our family.

"Dylan, you're home early! I hope they didn't kick you out," Dad said, smiling, stepping over the stuff he and Scottie had dumped in the entryway. They'd been at a banquet for the end of Scottie's soccer camp.

"Ha ha, Dad," I said, rolling my eyes and giving him a hug.

"They, um, didn't actually kick you out, right?" he asked, looking worried.

"No!"

"Does this girl have a story for you," said Mom. "You won't believe it."

We sat around the island in the kitchen, eating chips, and Dad and Scottie listened with gaped mouths as I told them about the last few weeks.

Dad was somewhat less impressed with what I'd done. "Why would you want to go spend time with those sort of people?" he asked. "There's a whole world of people out there, and you go hang out with the crazies?"

"They're not crazy, Dad," I said. "Well, not most of them. They just have different … priorities. And beliefs. And ways of living."

"And chickens," said Scottie, who thought living on a farm sounded kind of awesome.

"Yes, and chickens." I smiled at him.

Dad looked at Mom. "So, are we going to punish her for this or what?"

Mom shrugged. "Well, you know, in the grand scheme of things she could have done, this doesn't exactly qualify as horrible. Did you learn any valuable lessons?" she asked me.

"I think so," I said. "Lying for that long is terrible and it hurts people."

Mom nodded. "Anything else?"

I thought of Abigail. It was eight p.m. right now, which meant she would be cleaning up from dinner, whirling around the kitchen with her mom and Chastity. Beau would probably be there. I shivered.

"I'm really, really thankful for my life," I said.

"You're not going to want to go to church all the time, are you?" Dad asked nervously. "You weren't, like, converted into a cult or anything, right?"

I shook my head. "I don't think organized religion is for me. At least, not like that."

Dad looked relieved.

"I mean, it would be nice to believe in something," I said. "I was … jealous of that. I guess."

Mom and Dad glanced at each other again.

"We believe in things," said Dad, defensively.

"Such as?" I asked.

"Well…" he looked uncomfortable. "Hard work and discipline and…"

He trailed off, looking at Mom for help.

"Being an honorable and hardworking person," she said. "And being loyal to your family. And accepting people the way they are."

I nodded. "Those are all good things."

"Love," Mom said, putting her arms around both Scottie and me. "We believe in love."

"Gross," said Scottie, wrinkling his nose as Mom kissed his head.

"Don't you feel like our family values those things?" Mom asked. "I mean, we don't go around talking about it all the time—"

"I know," I said. "I think maybe I just… forgot about it. Maybe we could talk about it more."

Mom sighed. "We'll work harder at it, Pickle. We'll try."

"It's never too late to change, I guess," I said, smiling at them.

TWENTY-EIGHT

Mom hadn't been kidding about taking the summer off, and we started going regularly to a kickboxing class at the gym. After more than a week of bustling around at the Deans', I was amazed by how awake I felt compared to before the trip. Even if my brain was wild and confused with everything that had happened, my body had certainly appreciated the time not spent sitting in front of a computer like an inert blob.

The class instructor yelled at us, urging us to work harder, to grunt and yell as we went through the routine. She told us to imagine we were fighting someone we hated.

I put Beau's face in the line of my fist as I punched. I imagined Mr. Dean at the receiving end of my foot. It was very satisfying.

One day in early August, a few weeks after I'd gotten

home, Mom and I were walking out to the parking lot after class, laughing as we compared notes.

And that's when I saw Amanda.

She'd seen me first and was hanging back by her car, fidgeting with her keys and watching me with a nervous expression on her face.

A month before, I would have walked on by, acting like I hadn't seen her. I would have been certain she was judging and hating me, remembering details of my appearance to gossip over with Kelsey. Or that she was scared to be seen with me.

Basically, I would have assumed the worst.

But this time, after telling Mom I'd meet her at the car, I walked right up to my old friend. Her eyes got bigger and bigger as I got closer.

"Hey, Amanda," I said, smiling.

For a second, I was afraid she wouldn't respond. But then she smiled back, looking just as amazed as I was that this interaction was happening.

"Oh, um, hey Dylan. What's up?"

"How's your summer going?"

She giggled nervously and then said, "It's okay, I guess. You?"

"Well, it's been mighty weird," I said with a laugh. "To say the least."

It was so bizarre, as if no time had passed between that moment and the last time we'd talked like friends. At the party, right before everything changed.

"You … you look good!" she said. "Like you've been … getting out?"

She cringed as she finished her sentence, as if realizing how it could be construed as bitchy. Anyone would be able to guess that since the Blake thing, I hadn't been getting out much.

But I just smiled and nodded, letting it go. "You could say that."

"So … " she said, looking down at her feet.

"So … " I said.

"Dylan, I just—" she said, at the same time that I blurted out, "Can I say something?"

We both stopped and laughed.

"You first," I said.

"Well, I just … " She hesitated. "I'm glad I ran into you, because I just wanted to say that I feel really bad about what you went through last year. Like, really really bad? Especially since school's been out and I've had more time to sit around and think about it. What happened to you was awful and … I should've figured out how to be there for you. I'm just … I'm just really sorry, and I was wondering if … and I know it's kind of a long shot … but if you'd maybe forgive me?"

She searched my face anxiously, obviously worried about how I would react. But in my head, there was only one possible way to respond to what Amanda had just said. I stepped forward and threw my arms around her. She laughed with relief and hugged me back.

"I'm sorry, too!" I said, surprised at how familiar it felt

to hug her again. "I was terrible to you and Kelsey at that party. And I was terrible after it, too. I mean, you guys were so right about Blake and I didn't want to listen to you because I was so stubborn and ... and prideful."

We stepped away from each other, and I was surprised to see tears in her eyes.

"After that happened," she said, "I really wanted to have your back, but ... well ... "

I remembered the time in the hallway. When Amanda had tried to make peace but I'd walked away and not allowed her to finish.

"I didn't really want my back to be had," I said, cringing. "I was pretty pissed off at the world."

"Who can blame you?" she burst out sympathetically. "After what that pathetic excuse for a person did to you? Anyone would be angry, right?"

I nodded. "He's basically the worst thing ever."

"Totally. The absolute worst."

We stood there for a moment, both sunny and smiling at each other in our moment of reconciliation, but then I had to ask.

"How does Kelsey feel about all of this? And me?"

Amanda's face clouded a bit.

"Oh, you know her," Amanda said. "She kind of—"

"Holds grudges?" I suggested. "Like an elephant?"

"Yep," she replied. "But I know she misses you, you know? There have been all these times when we're talking and she starts to say something about 'remember when we…' and then she trails off and gets sad and I know she's thinking about you."

"I think about her, too. About both of you," I said, finally letting a wave of longing for my old friends pass over me. I tried to push away the conflicted feelings I still had—where had they been when things were getting thrown at my head in class? When people were writing stuff on my locker and sending me cruel emails? They'd been avoiding me. Pretending I didn't exist.

It was almost like Amanda was reading my mind. She'd always been so good at that, defusing the situation.

"Dyl, you should have seen how pissed Kelsey got at people who said nasty things about you," she said. "After those pictures came out, I had to talk her out of going after Blake with a baseball bat, you know? She heard about some guys who were going to toilet paper your house, and told them she'd destroy them all if so much as one square ended up in your yard."

She gave a short laugh. "One time, we came into school early to try and scrub some of that stuff off your locker that people kept writing. We almost got it all cleaned off, too."

I stared at her, wondering how it was possible I hadn't known any of this.

"But…" I said dumbly, "why didn't you…"

"Kelsey didn't want you to know about it," Amanda said with a shrug. "She was…well, we were both still hurt and didn't think you wanted us around. We were waiting for you to come back to us. To...you know, be honest with us?"

I pursed my lips, trying to process this new information. It felt like the world was shifting and things were becoming clearer.

"Can we fix this?" I asked Amanda. "I mean, for-real fix it, not just gloss it over and pretend-everything-is-okay-when-it's-really-not fix it? I'll totally take half the blame, too. All the blame, if I have to."

She looked at me and smiled. "I'm sure we can figure it out."

. . .

We arranged a peace summit for the next evening, at the diner where we used to hang out all the time back when things were normal. Amanda didn't tell Kelsey I was going to be there, and when Kelsey walked into the restaurant and saw me sitting in the booth, I could see how much she just wanted to turn around and walk right out again.

"Kels, over here!" said Amanda brightly.

Reluctantly, like twenty-pound weights were tied to both her ankles, Kelsey trudged over and slid into the booth next to Amanda.

"Hey," I said.

"Hi," she replied, picking up the menu and pretending to be absorbed in it.

I left her alone for a moment, knowing she'd need

some time to adjust to this turn of events. Kelsey didn't do well with surprises even in the best of times.

Eventually she slammed her menu down on the table and openly glared at me.

"So what's this all about?" she said, her dark eyes flashing.

Amanda told her about running into me the day before and how we'd talked and made up. "It was all just a stupid, stubborn misunderstanding, right?" she concluded. "No one's fault, exactly, just stupid. And it's gone on way too long, hasn't it?"

Kelsey and I were having a little impromptu staring contest. I blinked first, on purpose, and she looked momentarily triumphant.

"But you started it, Dylan," Kelsey said. "You told us we were jealous when we were just trying to protect you from that douchenozzle. And then you ignored us, your best friends. It was like we didn't exist. Seeing you walk through the halls with him was like … like … it was really awful."

There was pain in her voice. And since Kelsey was not the type to ever show pain if she could help it, I knew it was a big deal. She meant it.

My first instinct was still to get defensive. To declare they hadn't been supportive of me, and that they'd totally deserted me in my hour of need. An irrational part of me was still feeling betrayed and in pain and wanted to take it out on them, wanted to make them feel guilty about what had happened.

Then another part of me spoke, with something that sounded like Abigail's voice. *Forgive.*

I thought of all the times the three of us had stood up for each other, when we were our indestructible little force to be reckoned with. I thought about what Amanda had said, the covert ways they'd stuck up for me that I hadn't even known about.

And I thought of Abigail, out in that garden, thinking she had no friends and no choices. And here I was, with all the choices in the world. And with friends who loved me and had my back, even when I'd been convinced I was alone.

I swallowed hard. "You're right," I told Kelsey. "You were just trying to protect me, and I blew you off. And I was too stubborn to back down, even when it was obvious he was indeed a ... douche."

I reached out and grabbed both their hands where they were lying on the table.

"I'm sorry," I said, my voice cracking. "I love you both and I hope you guys can forgive me."

Amanda squeezed my hand immediately, and then looked over at Kelsey.

Kelsey looked down at our hands for a moment, and then up at my face. She seemed to fight a brief inner battle, and then, slowly, she smiled and squeezed my hand.

"So when do we begin to plan our Blake revenge?" she asked. "Because I have some ideas. What are your feelings about flame throwers?"

A wave of relief swept over me and I giggled, feeling lighter than I had in almost a year. I could face the school halls again. Hell, I could face the whole world again, as long as they were on my side.

My friends ... my awesome friends.

"I'm in firm favor of flame throwers, and I want to hear all of the ideas," I said. "But can I just tell you guys this crazy story first?"

TWENTY-NINE

I drove home singing along to the radio, feeling giddy about the reconciliations with Kelsey and Amanda and all the talking we'd done. I'd told them almost everything about my trip to the Deans', even some of the parts that I hadn't told my parents. Such as kissing Asher.

"Scandal!" Kelsey had said, her eyes wide. She gave me an appreciative fist bump.

Amanda wasn't so convinced. "Dylan, you don't honestly think that—"

"I don't think anything about him," I said. "I mean, we don't even really know each other that well. I bet he's already engaged to some nice, appropriate girl in Georgia or something. I'll probably see his wedding pictures on Abigail's blog in a few months."

"So you're not … hoping?" Amanda asked, her eyebrows

raised. "That he'll come around some day? Even though you guys have such different lives?"

"Um, chill out, Amanda," Kelsey said. "He sounds like a much better person than the last asshole. At least Asher has, like, *morals*."

"Still," said Amanda, looking at me, concerned.

"Honestly, guys," I said. "I think I've got my head screwed on straight for this one. And if I freak out and get all obsessed and irrational, I give you both full permission to smack me and remind me of this conversation. And then smack me again if necessary."

They glanced at each other, and then smiled at me.

"You're on," said Kelsey, and we all shook on it.

"Enough about all my nonsense," I said. "What's been going on with you guys? Tell me everything."

When I got home, I said hi to my mom, who was working in the living room on her improbable new hobby of scrapbooking, and then ran up to my room. I went straight to my computer to check my email.

Earlier in the day, I'd posted my last Faith blog entry. I'd only posted sporadic and impersonal things since coming back from Abigail's, unsure of what to do with the site. Even though I'd promised Abigail I'd end it, I was hesitant about outright shutting it down with no explanation. But making up new fake Faith stories wasn't right either. I felt like I owed something to my readers, but I couldn't figure out what it might be.

As the days wore on, I'd started to feel more and more … dirty and deceitful about continuing the story.

Knowing that there was someone out there, Abigail, who knew the truth and who had been hurt by my lies. I had to follow through with my promise.

So, that very morning, I'd decided it was time to shut the site down once and for all.

It was definitely hard to do, since it felt like deleting a whole part of my personality. Or cutting off a limb with a rusty saw.

But I'd gritted my teeth, removed all the archives, and pounded out one last entry, determined to leave gracefully. In my floweriest language, I'd thanked everyone for reading and told them I was excited and encouraged to pursue other activities.

> *I've been very blessed by our fellowship on this site,* I wrote, which was actually totally true. *I've learned more than I ever thought possible, and I've found my happy ending. I wish you all the very best in life. Goodbye!*

In the comments, my readers had immediately started to speculate that I was quitting the blog because I'd gotten engaged. Since that, of course, was the only possible happy ending for a girl like Faith. They begged and pleaded for more details, but I didn't respond, even though new ideas for the next chapter of Faith's life involuntarily flooded into my brain.

I was done with faking Faith.

But maybe I could put it in a novel…

That night, I swiftly clicked through the comment notifications in my email inbox, one by one, but stopped cold when I saw something from Abigail. Despite everything that had happened, she was apparently still checking my blog. And for one terrified moment, I thought maybe she was going to out me to all the readers and create the second public Internet scandal of my life.

But, no ... it was just an email directly to me. Abigail hadn't commented publicly.

She'd addressed the email to Faith, despite the fact that she knew that girl didn't exist. It was like she was writing to a ghost.

> *Is it sad that I'm going to miss your blog, even though I know now that everything you wrote was completely made up? It was like finally meeting a kindred spirit, this girl who seemed to know what my life was like, who wrote so genuinely. There are other blogs out there, I know, but yours somehow felt the most real. I wish you were real. I didn't feel so alone. But I guess that makes me silly.*

It was near midnight and she'd sent it only a few minutes before, at a time when I knew everyone else in her house would be in bed. I imagined her sitting in the little computer room in her pink nightgown, the dark house pressing down around her. I wanted to reach through the screen and give her a hug.

But all I could do was reply to her email.

*Always remember that I will come and get you, no
questions asked. I have your back.*

And I included my phone number.

I thought there was a good chance she'd just delete
my email, but it didn't hurt to say it one last time. Maybe
someday, if my darkest worries about Beau were confirmed
and she found herself in a bad spot, she would remember
my promise.

Almost immediately, as if she'd been sitting there waiting for my reply, another email arrived in my inbox.

*Just so you know, Asher left the farm in Georgia
where Daddy took him just a few days after he got
there. He left a note that he was going to travel for a
while, and no one's heard from him for a couple of
weeks. If you happen to see him, please let me know
he's okay. We miss him.*

I stared at the words on the screen for a while, my
heart pounding, trying to comprehend.

Asher had actually broken away from his family! Was
he on his way to Chicago to find me? If he'd left weeks
ago, why hadn't he gotten here yet? Where was he?

Wasn't he looking for me?

The note he'd written on that last morning was sitting
in my top desk drawer. I took it out and traced the words
with my finger for a while, something I'd been doing almost
every night since I'd gotten home. Despite what I'd said to
Kelsey and Amanda about being totally casual regarding

Asher, my heart still hurt. And all I wanted was more time with him. That didn't seem like too much to ask.

But even with this new information, his message was just as vague and maddening.

Dylan,

As soon as I deserve you, I will come and find you.

Love, Asher

What did that mean? We were both screwed-up, flawed people with regrets and weird histories. Why didn't we deserve each other *now*? What could he possibly be out there looking for?

There wasn't any way for me to know the answer. I'd only drive myself crazy.

After a while, I put the note away, shut my computer down, and looked around my lavender room. Mom and I had gone shopping for some new white bedding, and my space was cozy and clean and cheerful, even at night. It felt more like a place I could be content than my old room ever had.

I'd washed my modest clothes from the trip to Abigail's and they were all sitting in a heap in my closet, waiting for me to figure out what to do with them. I took out the pink nightgown with the silly bow at the collar that Abigail had given me and put it on. It felt soft and familiar on my skin.

Before I drifted off to sleep, I thought of Asher and his words. I couldn't picture where he was or what he was doing. He had no Internet presence, so I couldn't stalk him online. I couldn't call him. I couldn't email him. I couldn't go physically looking for him. All I could do was keep living my life, try to figure it all out, and hope that maybe someday I'd see him again.

But with my whole full heart, I tried to send waves of love and acceptance to wherever Asher was sleeping that night.

"You're amazing," I whispered into my dark room. "And you deserve to be happy."

And for the first time I could remember, I fell asleep peacefully.

Adam P. Schweigert

About the Author

Josie Bloss grew up in East Lansing, Michigan. She attended the University of Michigan in Ann Arbor and the University of St. Andrews in Scotland. When not mining her high school journals for material, Josie enjoys obsessing over various TV shows, karaoke, and all things theater. She lives in Bloomington, Indiana.